Just
Perfect
GRACE TURNER

I0834298

contents

Author's Note vii

Prologue 1
Chapter 1 7
Chapter 2 11
Chapter 3 17
Chapter 4 23
Chapter 5 27
Chapter 6 31
Chapter 7 39
Chapter 8 45
Chapter 9 51
Chapter 10 57
Chapter 11 63
Chapter 12 67
Chapter 13 71
Chapter 14 77
Chapter 15 83
Chapter 16 89
Chapter 17 93
Chapter 18 101
Chapter 19 107
Chapter 20 113
Epilogue 121

Acknowledgments 125
Also By Grace Turner 127
About the Author 129

To anyone who has ever wanted two boyfriends who are also boyfriends.

author's note

This book is intended for adults and contains sexually explicit situations. It's really just a spicy, romantic good time.

If you have any questions about the content of this book, please feel free to email me at graceturnerauthor@gmail.com or send me a message @graceturnerauthor on Instagram.

Happy reading!!

prologue

. . .

Liam

10 years earlier

The pounding beat of the music vibrated through my chest as I tilted the beer bottle to my lips. I didn't want to be there, but I'd promised my best friend, Easton, I'd come for a little while.

Although he was nowhere to be found, and I was relegated to a corner waiting for him.

Parties—in particular frat parties—weren't my scene. But there wasn't much I wouldn't do for him. I'd stay for the least amount of time possible, though. I had to keep my scholarship to pay for school, and I needed to keep my grades up to make that happen. I couldn't pay for tuition and books without it, and spending the night drinking and partying before a big test wasn't a great idea. One failed test could fuck up everything.

Standing in a corner close to the door leading to the back patio, I lifted my beer to my lips again as someone else came to stand near me.

"I hope you don't mind," the gorgeous brunette said, just loud enough to be heard over the music. "I'm meeting someone, but I don't really want to be a part of *that*." She motioned to the chaos and throng of bodies several feet away.

My breath caught the second I got a good look at her. Long, brown hair fell over her shoulders, and wide brown eyes looked up at me. Her jeans and black tee were tight, like they were painted on her skin and showed off every little dip and curve of her body.

Fuck, she was perfect. And her smile was contagious. It warmed my skin and made me feel special to be on the receiving end of it.

"I don't mind at all," I said, wiping the condensation from my hand onto my jeans before I extended it to her. "I'm Liam."

She glanced down, and her smile widened when she took my hand. It was smaller than mine, but she gave it one good, firm shake. Electricity speared up my arm, and I didn't want to ever let go.

Her mouth dropped open like she felt it too, and we stood there for the length of another breath, holding hands and each other's gaze.

I was mustering up the courage to let her hand go when someone bumped into me, and it happened anyway. I dropped her hand and stepped between them, blocking the guy from shoving into her.

"Oh, shit, man," the guy slurred, bracing his hands on my chest to find his balance. "I'm so sorry." He tapped me twice and stumbled off.

Once he was gone, I moved back.

"You okay?" I asked, looking her up and down.

"Yeah, I'm fine. Thanks."

She smiled and sipped her drink.

"I don't think I caught your name."

She swallowed and licked the excess liquid off her lips. "Palmer. I'm Palmer."

A pretty name for such a pretty girl. "It's nice to meet you, Palmer."

"It's nice to meet you too, Liam. So…are you usually a wallflower?"

I laughed and shrugged. "I guess you could say that. My roommate is forever worried about my social life, so I promised him I would come for a little while."

"Does he have a reason to be worried?"

She leaned back against the table in front of me and crossed her arms over her chest. It took more willpower than I wanted to admit not to glance down at her tits. Quickly doing the math, I realized it had been months since I'd last gotten laid. But that wasn't abnormal for me. I didn't relish in the occasional hook-up like many of my friends. I was a one-person guy.

Palmer was different, though. The sudden attraction was swift and consuming—something I'd only experienced once before and a feeling I'd never actually acted on. Only in my head and in the privacy of my bedroom, with the door locked and no one else home, did I let those fantasies free.

"No, he doesn't have a reason to be worried. It's not like I'm a hermit or a shut-in. He just prefers this kind of thing more than I do."

"So, he's the life-of-the-party type and you're…" She trailed off, and I felt her eyes sweep over me. "The more quiet and reserved of you two?"

Her assumption was accurate. *Very* accurate. "Exactly," I confirmed.

She nodded and took a long sip of her drink, eyes darting around the crowd of people like she was looking for someone.

"I don't think there's anything wrong with that."

I smiled at the sincerity that laced her voice and shone bright in her eyes when she finally looked back at me. She was my ideal woman in every way imaginable, and I felt lucky just being in her presence.

"You don't? You should tell him that then. I'd love the backup."

She tilted her head back and laughed toward the ceiling. I

watched her throat work and was mesmerized at the sound I could barely hear above the music and the long line of her neck. I caught myself wondering how she'd feel beneath my hands, how she'd smell, or how she'd look tangled up in my sheets.

"I think the idea of both is nice. I enjoy the outgoing, personable guy, but there's also something very appealing about the broody, quiet guy too."

It wasn't so much what she said but how she said it that made my cock thicken. Suddenly lightheaded from all the blood rushing below my belt, I thought I was seeing things when her eyes appraised me once again. A slow perusal of my body, I worried my erection would be obvious behind my jeans. God, I wanted her something fierce. And when her stare locked on mine, I clocked the desire stirring behind her eyes too.

My imagination—always so wild and uninhibited—conjured up glorious images in a single instant. Images of me lifting her and setting her down on the table behind her, stepping between her legs, and pressing my cock against her pussy. I could almost feel the heat with just the thought. Then I'd slam my mouth down on hers and feel her moan vibrate against my lips.

I could almost taste her on my tongue.

One half step forward, and I prepared to close the distance. My thoughts were singular, and she moved toward me too, until she was gone.

In the flash of an eye, Palmer was lifted into another man's arms, and he was kissing her neck.

No, not just another man's. Easton, my best friend and roommate, appeared and grabbed her, twirling her in the air and kissing her neck and cheek until she was giggling.

Both breathless, he set her back down and flashed his panty-dropping grin at me, then glanced down at her.

"Looks like you met Liam," he said, tucking her hair behind her ear.

Realization simultaneously dawned on us both. It felt like a bucket of ice water over my head, seeping through to my bones.

"I didn't realize—" she said, clearing her throat and shaking her head like it was supposed to remove the shock from her expression. "Liam is your roommate you've been talking about."

And Palmer was "P," the woman Easton had become infatuated with in just a few short weeks.

What were the fucking odds?

My heart broke, but I schooled my features. Palmer's eyes caught mine just before I looked away. Pretending not to see the apology I knew was poised on her tongue, she turned back to Easton and smiled up at him.

I scanned the party and ignored the couple kissing behind me as well as the deep pang in my chest—not just for the woman I couldn't have, but for the man too.

one

. . .

Liam

Present day

I SHOULD HAVE BEEN EXCITED. A four-day vacation in the Colorado mountains with my favorite people on the planet sounded perfect.

But pulling up to the sprawling resort, all I could think about was how miserable I was about to be.

I'd been a third wheel for most of our adult lives. Ever since Palmer and Easton started dating in college, I'd been *their* plus one. But this trip was supposed to be different.

And it was going to be until a few hours ago.

I'd been seeing Nicole for several months, and this was supposed to be our first trip together. But instead of meeting me at the airport like we'd planned, she'd called me as I stood by the security entrance and told me she wasn't coming.

Not only that she wasn't coming, but that she didn't want to be with me anymore.

Although I'd felt her pulling away recently, I'd hoped it was all in my head. A few months together, and I knew her better than that. It was like a switch flipped a few weeks ago, and it all came to a head right then.

So I had a decision to make—tell my best friends I was no longer coming or be the third wheel yet again. I didn't know why I even pretended like it was a decision when there was only one answer.

Without much family of my own, they had more than welcomed me into theirs. Even before Easton met Palmer, his family took me in. I was just the teenager next door whose mom worked too much before she died and had no one else to turn to. But I wasn't without a family for long. I was with the Winters for every holiday, every trip, and everything in between from eighteen until now, at thirty-one.

When he'd married Palmer, that hadn't changed. We were together more than we were apart, living only down the street from each other.

There was no decision. I tucked my phone into my pocket and took a deep breath. The lack of pain in my chest was a sign that the breakup was for the best.

My heart didn't ache like it did when Easton proposed to Palmer. And my body didn't feel like it was going to collapse like when I stood beside him on their wedding day and had a front-row seat to Palmer's joy and elation.

That memory was at the forefront of my mind as my ride pulled to a stop at the front of the resort. Tucked into the side of the snow-covered mountains was The Lodge, a five-star resort and spa. The exterior was wood and natural stone, with tall trees surrounding the curved drive and old-timey lamp posts just beginning to turn on as the sun set over the mountain.

Grabbing my suitcase from the trunk, I slung my duffel over my shoulder and was met by a very eager attendant at the top of the stairs.

"Good evening. Welcome to The Lodge," he said, swinging the door open and waving me inside. It was warm, and I began to defrost.

Texas to Colorado was a huge difference, and I wasn't built for the cold, although I loved the scenery and the snow.

The natural, elevated log-cabin aesthetic continued into the interior with warm tones and leather accents. There was a stone fireplace with an impressive fire in the middle of the reception area, and I could feel the heat radiating off it as I made my way to the check-in desk.

The woman behind the counter was as nice as the attendant who opened the door for me. The check-in process was simple, and a few minutes later, she was handing me a pamphlet of the amenities and giving me directions to the elevators.

With only two bags, I declined her offer to have another attendant escort me to my room. When the elevator doors closed, my nerves doubled. By the time they were opening on our floor, my body was buzzing with them.

Easton had booked us adjoining rooms, so we didn't have to worry about possibly being on opposite sides of the resort. It seemed like a good idea when there were four of us, but now, it would mean that I'd be forced to listen to them have amazing sex for four fucking days.

I'd have to find earplugs. Or consider surgery to remove my ability to hear altogether.

Halfway down the hallway, I found my room—612. A housekeeper pushed a cart full of cleaning supplies past me, and I gave her a small smile as I waved the key card over the pad and heaved open the heavy door.

Inside, it took me a second to find the light switch, but when I did, the entire hallway was illuminated in warm light. I dropped my bag and wandered farther in.

There was a small seating area with a leather couch and a small wooden chair off the entryway. To the right was the bathroom with gold finishes and not only a claw-foot tub, but a rainfall shower that I needed more than anything.

At the end of the hallway, the room opened up. On the right side, a large king-sized bed with all-white linens sat against the wall. A TV bigger than any I had in my house sat opposite it, and twin wood bedside tables sat next to it.

But the most amazing part was the view. The back of the room was all floor-to-ceiling sliding glass doors that looked out onto the back of the property and the mountain.

Between the time I'd gotten out of my car and walked to my room, it had begun snowing, and the lights scattered around the property, lining every walkway and hanging among the trees, were beautiful.

My breath fogged up the glass as I stood in awe and stared at the view before me. If it hadn't been so cold, I would have ventured out onto the patio for a closer look.

Palmer was a marketing executive, and Easton was a highly sought after architect, so they were used to a little more luxury. For me, this was a once-in-a-decade splurge. As an electrician, I made good money, but it wasn't nearly as much as their dual-income household.

Walking back toward the front of the room where I'd dropped my bags, I eyed the door next to the oversized TV. The door I knew for certain would lead into Easton and Palmer's room.

I stopped and considered whether I should knock or text them that I'd arrived.

I'd told them I was on my way an hour ago from the airport, and they'd both responded with how excited they were to see *us.* Yeah, they didn't know yet, because I was too chickenshit to tell them another relationship had failed and that their dream of couples' activities had yet again shattered.

I ran a frustrated hand through my unruly blond mop and let my head fall back. I took a long, deep breath and groaned quietly.

Still contemplating what to do next, I didn't have to make the decision. A faint knock came from the other side of the door, and my pulse raced with anticipation.

two

Palmer

LAUGHING, I fumbled for the key card and slid it against the pad to open the door to our hotel room.

Behind me, I heard Easton's deep chuckle and glanced back to find him shaking his head. We'd booked an earlier flight, so we had some time to kill before Liam and Nicole arrived.

We decided to walk around the resort and ended up finding a beautiful bar in one of the other buildings. A couple of whiskeys later, and I couldn't stop giggling at everything.

I wasn't drunk, but I was just this side of tipsy, where everything was funny, and I felt light on my feet.

"Should I make you some coffee to sober up?" Easton asked, helping me pull off my large winter coat. My hand got stuck, and I shook it hard a few times to yank it free. That triggered another giggle fit. "Never mind, I'm definitely making you coffee," he said. He hung our coats on the rack by the door as I wandered farther into the room.

"Always taking such good care of me," I said, turning to find Easton standing at the coffeemaker, reading the little pamphlet of instructions for the contraption. It was fancier than anything we had at home, yet somehow had fewer buttons.

His dark brows furrowed as he read, and I stopped to take him in.

My husband was fucking hot, and somehow, I only grew more attracted to him. I didn't think it was possible, but just looking at him made me question whether we had enough time for a quickie before our friends arrived.

He was tall and toned with dark hair I loved to run my fingers through, and it was just long enough to grab and tug. His sharp jaw was dusted with dark hair that he kept trimmed shorter because he knew I preferred his beard that way.

Not to mention he was kind and thoughtful and loving, and genuinely a good person. But all those qualities were secondary to my tipsy, horny brain that was more enthralled with the curve of his tight, perky ass and the impressive cock trapped behind his pants than his caring nature.

"If you don't stop looking at me like that, P, we're never going to make it to dinner."

I hadn't even realized he'd caught me staring, and he didn't look up as he spoke, like he could just feel me watching him.

Ten years together and five years married, we were like that —communicating without words and anticipating the other's next move or needs. It was a privilege to know someone that well.

"I can't help it," I sighed wistfully. A few steps, and I stood next to him, leaning my hip against the little coffee bar and looking up at his amused expression. "My husband is just so hot."

Green eyes finally flashed to mine, and before I could register what was happening, Easton wrapped a hand around my throat and pushed me up against the wall next to us. My back hit the unforgiving surface, and I huffed out a surprised breath.

His fingers squeezed my throat just enough to make it a little harder to find my next breath, but I smiled up at him as he loomed over me. In complete contradiction to his domineering demeanor, he placed a sweet kiss on my forehead before he dropped his mouth to my ear.

"And my wife is such a pretty little slut who can't go even a day without her husband's cock."

Licking my lips, my smile widened, and I tilted my head to run my nose against his cheek.

"Because it's such a good cock," I whispered. Easton groaned and dropped his mouth to my neck, just beneath his thumb, as he ground his hips against me, proving that he was just as affected as I was.

I'd won the lottery with him. Not only was he a good person, but he also had a magnificent dick that did insanely dirty and depraved things to me.

I opened my mouth to tell him we could be late to dinner when there was a sound from the other room, the room that was connected to ours for Liam and Nicole.

My pulse jumped like it always did when Liam was around. Every time I saw him, I remembered that first night I met him at that party, when he was standing against the wall, looking very out of place with a scowl and a nearly full beer.

It was the second time I'd ever felt that fluttering feeling, like I was jumping off a building without a parachute. The first time I'd felt it was when I'd met Easton, and I'd never gotten over the way the two men gave me butterflies.

Easton glanced around the corner at the door.

"They must be here," I said, and he nodded, stepping back and readjusting his erection.

I laughed and kissed him quickly. "I'll take care of that later. Promise."

Easton muttered something about me being a tease—which we both knew was completely untrue—while I knocked quickly on the door to the other room. A few seconds later, I heard the lock on the other side click before the door swung open, revealing a slightly disheveled Liam.

But I didn't care what he looked like. He was here.

"You're here!" I exclaimed, not hesitating to jump and hug him. He caught me, and I felt him chuckle as he hugged me back, careful to hold my back and upper thigh rather than grab my ass.

Liam was large and broad. It was an effort to jump into his arms, but he held me like I weighed nothing.

"Hey, Sparky," he laughed.

After a second, he put me down and looked me over. "You a little drunk?"

I shook my head and rolled my eyes, gesturing with my thumb and forefinger that I was just a little tipsy.

Liam rolled his lips to hold in his laugh, then looked over my head at Easton. He scraped a hand across the light brown scruff covering his sharp jaw.

"Yeah, she's drunk. We found a bar while waiting for you and Nicole."

Glancing around the room and not finding Liam's girlfriend, I looked back at him. "Umm…where *is* Nicole?"

Liam's entire demeanor immediately changed. He straightened and dragged a hand through his dirty blond hair as he blew out a long breath. I could feel his anxiety like it were my own, and I sucked in a deep breath. It was second nature to reach out and comfort him with a hand on his arm. Really, I wanted to do more.

"She's still in Dallas," he said, and I looked over my shoulder at Easton, whose expression bore the same confusion I was sure mine did.

"Did she miss her flight?" Easton asked, and Liam shook his head.

"No, she broke up with me while I was waiting for her at the airport. Called me and just said it was over."

"Oh, no," I said, covering my mouth with my hand, and immediately feeling an overwhelming need to comfort him and make sure he was okay. We'd helped Liam through many a breakup before, but Nicole was his longest relationship in a while. And he seemed happy. I wanted him to be happy, but I struggled with my warring emotions.

I hated seeing him unhappy, but part of me was excited not to have to share him with someone else. Well, other than my husband.

"Shit, man. I'm so sorry," Easton said, stepping around me to comfort his best friend. He put a hand on his shoulder and squeezed once. Liam looked up, and I watched his shoulders drop and overall mood shift.

"Thanks, but I think it was for the best. She had started pulling away the past two weeks, so I can't say I'm entirely surprised. We're just not right for each other."

Reaching forward, I laced my fingers through Liam's. He looked down and smiled at the gesture.

"I'm okay. I promise. I don't want this to ruin your trip. I didn't even know whether I should still come or—"

"It won't ruin *our* trip. It's your trip too," Easton quickly clarified.

"And we're so glad you still came," I added.

Liam nodded, and I let go of his hand as he walked toward where his bags were lying beside the door. "Guess I'm back to third wheeling," he said with a chuckle. But I could hear the emotion he tried to disguise with humor.

Easton cut his eyes in my direction, confirming he'd heard it too.

I searched for the right words as Liam continued, "Dinner at eight, right?"

"Yeah, we have reservations at the main restaurant on the first floor," Easton said.

Liam dropped his suitcase on the luggage rack and began to unzip it. "Cool. I'll shower and meet you guys down there."

"Okay, we'll let you get settled," I said, reaching for Easton. "We'll see you in a few."

Liam nodded, and Easton and I shuffled back into our room, closing the door behind us but not worrying to lock it.

"Fuck," Easton cursed, scrubbing a hand over his jaw. "I didn't see this coming."

"I know, but he seems to be taking it pretty well."

"He does," he muttered. Remembering my coffee, he grabbed a sugar and creamer, dumping both in before handing it to me. It was still slightly warm and tasted great for hotel room coffee. "He just...he deserves so much more. I know he wants to find someone and settle down. I just don't understand why it hasn't happened yet."

In the moment, I blamed what I said next on the lingering effects of the alcohol still present in my bloodstream. Or maybe that I was fully relaxed and unburdened for the first time in what felt like months.

Both of those things were true, but they alone weren't enough. It was the years of wondering, of observing the two of them together, that I really blamed. Or the desire thick in my blood from the thought.

"Maybe it hasn't happened because the person he really wants is...you."

three

. . .

Easton

I WHIPPED AROUND SO FAST I almost lost my balance, but Palmer was staring up at me, innocently holding her coffee cup between her hands like she hadn't just dropped one hell of a bomb.

"What?" I croaked out, overcome with a wave of emotions I couldn't even begin to sort through. One second, I'm trying to console my best friend after a breakup, and in the next, my wife, my perfect other half, was questioning if I was the reason for all his past failed relationships.

She shrugged and took another sip of her drink. "It's just a thought, babe. One that I've had a time…or twenty."

"Twenty?" I scoffed.

She held up her hand and shook her head. "Actually, you're right. My number is off a little bit. I consider it almost every single time the two of you are together."

Palmer and I had no secrets. It was something we'd agreed early on in our relationship, especially once we'd decided that we were going to get married one day. No matter how bad it seemed, we'd talk it out. And it worked well for us thus far.

Except that was a really big secret she'd kept from me.

"Sweetheart, you've lost it. That's not—it can't be…"

As I stuttered over my words, her eyebrows raised, and she shot me her best incredulous look.

But two could play that game. I crossed my arms over my chest and pushed my nerves aside.

"Or maybe it's you?"

Unlike me, Palmer skipped shock and went straight to laughter. She was laughing so hard that she had to wipe away a few stray tears before she could speak again.

"You're funny," she said, shaking her head and taking another long sip of her coffee.

"Occasionally, I am, but right now, I'm being serious. And I don't think it's one-sided."

At that, she stopped and suddenly became very serious.

"In case you forgot, I *love* you. I married *you*." She set her coffee cup on the dresser and stabbed her finger at the ring on her opposite hand. The large engagement ring I'd saved forever for. The one that made her cry when I'd finally dropped down on one knee.

"I'm not—" My words quickly cut off, and I realized we were arguing right next to the door that led to Liam's room. It wasn't necessarily a conversation I thought he should be privy to. Yet.

"Come here," I said, grabbing Palmer's hand and tugging her down the hallway and into the bathroom. I closed the door behind us and turned to find her standing in the middle of the room with her hands on her hips. "I didn't want him to overhear," I explained.

"Yes, yes, I get it. Now, please tell me you understand that you're my person."

In two easy steps, I closed the distance between us and braced my hands on either side of her face. Her head tipped back, and she instantly melted in my hold.

"Of course I understand that, sweet girl. You're the love of my life, and you never make me question how much you love me."

She smiled and glanced down at my mouth, but I was already going to kiss her. There was no way I couldn't. I pressed our lips together, and fuck, it was always like the first time. Nothing had ever felt so perfect. I'd never felt so complete.

Pulling away, I dropped my forehead to hers. "So I guess we're both saying the same thing."

"I guess we are."

"But I'm not sure what that means."

Palmer tilted her head back and dropped her hands to my chest. She picked a piece of lint off my shirt and sucked in a shaky breath as she looked back up at me. It wasn't often that I saw my usually confident and unshakable wife anxious.

"I think it doesn't mean anything unless we clarify one thing," she said slowly. Her eyes were steadfast on mine, and I knew she could feel my heart pounding beneath her hands.

"What is that?" I asked, running my thumb against her smooth cheek and watching her intently.

"Of course, we don't know what Liam thinks or if we're really correct in our assumptions about his possible feelings. But if we *are,* then we have to decide if it…goes both ways."

"If he goes both ways?" I asked, and Palmer coughed out a quick laugh and shook her head. I dropped my hands to clasp hers as I stepped back and gave her a little more space.

Liam had been open about his interest in both men and women, although he tended to date more women recently. It was one of the reasons we'd bonded in high school—two bisexual men going to public school in the South wasn't always easy.

Which was why I was confused by her statement.

"No, that's not what I said." She chuckled. "But I understand your confusion, and rather than talk in circles, I'm just going to be blunt, okay?"

I nodded, and she squeezed my hands.

"And no matter your answer, I know that you still love me, and I promise nothing will change between us, because I love you so much. And we—"

"P," I said quickly, effectively cutting off her rambling. "Just say it."

"If Liam does feel the way I think he does about you, would you return those feelings?"

The torrent of emotions was back, but even bigger and more wild.

Fifteen years of friendship wasn't anything to gawk at. I'd heard that if you're friends for more than seven years, you'll be friends forever. But I knew the moment Liam moved in next door, he would be a forever friend.

However, denying that there never was a thought that there could be something more felt wrong. I'd mentioned it to Palmer before, but I hadn't explained the entire story. With the current topic of conversation, it felt like a good time to fess up.

"I know I told you a while ago about how I thought that could be possible when we were younger," I began, and Palmer nodded, listening intently.

"When the whole thing with my dad happened."

Several years ago, Palmer's dad had a massive heart attack while I was traveling for work. We were newly married, and I felt like the worst husband in the world, not being able to be there. But Liam stepped up. He took her to the hospital and sat with her as long as she needed to.

When I finally got home the next day, Palmer confessed that she'd kissed Liam—that in her grief and terror that she'd lose her father, she found comfort in him.

I never felt betrayed or considered the possibility that she would leave me. Honestly, I was only ever happy with my best friend for being there for Palmer.

Liam and I talked about it afterward, and he was sincerely apologetic, promising that it ended as quickly as it started and that they both felt terrible.

When she told me about the kiss they shared, I probably should have told her about ours, but it didn't seem as relevant with her dad still in the hospital and her emotions in turmoil. All

I'd said at the time was that I understood Liam's pull and how, at one point, I thought there could have been more between us too.

"Right, but with everything that was happening at the time, I didn't give you the full story." Her brown eyes bounced between mine, but there was no judgment or anger behind them, which I was eternally thankful for. "When we were in high school, we kissed too."

Her eyes widened, but only for a moment before a sweet smile tilted her lips. "Really? I mean, I can't say I'm totally surprised. The idea that nothing ever happened felt a little far-fetched." She lifted onto her toes and kissed me gently. "Tell me about it."

"There's not much to tell. We were studying in his bedroom our senior year, talking about college and the future, when I just kissed him."

"Did he kiss you back?"

I nodded slowly, thinking back to that day and the two of us sitting on his bed. It was entirely the wrong way to go about it, but I was a horny teenager with a massive crush on my best friend. Finally, something just snapped, and I had to know what his lips felt like.

The memories of us together flashed behind my eyes—what it might have looked like from the outside looking in.

"How did it feel?" she asked, and her voice was a sultry whisper. My cock appreciated her tone and combined with the reminder of the one and only time I'd kissed Liam, I felt like I was about to explode.

"It felt…amazing," I sighed. Palmer's hand slipped down my stomach and cupped my erection, squeezing hard once and drawing a sharp gasp in turn. Her hand started to move, and her fingers tangled in the back of my hair.

"Tell me more."

four

. . .

Easton

I GROANED as she pumped me over the denim and tightened my hold on her hips.

"You kissed him, and then what happened?" she prompted.

"He, umm…he was surprised at first," I said, glancing down to watch her open my belt and slide my zipper down until she could reach inside my briefs and wrap her warm palm around my hard flesh.

"But he eventually relented, didn't he?"

I nodded, and she dug her nails into my shaft, wanting an answer more than a nod.

"Yes," I gasped, closing my eyes. "He kissed me back. He relaxed and let me lead the kiss. I pushed my tongue into his mouth and tasted him for the first and only time."

She moaned, and her hand was a vice around me. She pumped relentlessly, and I could already feel my release bearing down on me. Her skillful, delicate fingers knew exactly what to do. She knew exactly how to get me there, and fast.

"Did he touch you?"

"Yes," I hissed. "I held his face, and he grabbed my waist. But it ended so quickly. He pulled away."

"But what would you have preferred to happen? What do you want to happen now?"

Oh, fuck. There was no way I would last, thinking of every single fantasy I had of the three of us. There were too many to count.

The seed was already planted—I'd known for a long time that I still wanted Liam in a way I never thought possible. But with Palmer's coaxing, that seed was suddenly fully formed, strong and unwavering.

It gave me the strength to say what I'd barely let myself think, what I was too scared to ever admit aloud.

"I want all three of us. *Together,*" I growled. My balls tightened, and with one intentional squeeze to the crown of my cock, I came. It drenched Palmer's hand and landed on the front of her sweater, but she didn't stop pumping until the last drop pooled at the tip.

She let me go and lifted her hand to her mouth, licking off every drop while maintaining eye contact with me.

"Fuck, P," I groaned, and she smiled.

"For the record," she said, placing her other hand against my cheek and urging me to look at her. "I want that too. The three of us together sounds…perfect, like maybe that's the way it was supposed to be. But it doesn't take anything away from us."

Shaking my head, I caught my breath and held her closer. "Of course not. The foundation we built…I think it will only make it better."

"So, to be clear, we both want this? Not just a onetime thing, and not just sex. Like a relationship with all three of us?"

I didn't hesitate to answer. "Yes, that's what I want. But I also worry that it's going to fuck everything up. Losing our friendship or messing it up beyond repair…it would kill me."

"I know," she said. "I would hate that too. I know you've been friends for longer, but his friendship means the world to me too. And I don't know what it is exactly, but I have a feeling that won't happen. You two especially have been through a lot together. I don't think this is what will end things."

If nothing else, I believed in my wife. Her confidence stirred mine, and I really wanted her to be right.

She turned and flipped on the faucet, washing the final remnants of my cum from her hands. I took the moment to turn on the shower so I could start getting ready for dinner.

Stripping out of my jeans and shirt, I tossed them on the floor near the shower but looked back at Palmer before I hopped in the already steaming water.

"So what are we going to do? It's not really a topic that we can just bring up, right?"

"Yeah, I'm not so sure," she agreed. "Maybe it's the alcohol talking, but I might have a plan."

Her smile was so perfectly devious, my cock jumped in appreciation. She noted my reaction, and her laugh was all I ever needed to keep going.

"All I need from you is to tell me your limits. We need to talk about whether you're uncomfortable with anything involving the three of us. And then, I'll take it from there."

I swung the shower door open and stepped under the running water.

"I'm not sure what you mean by limits," I said, and she leaned against the glass shower door so I could see and hear her.

"Like, would you be comfortable with me kissing Liam?"

"Of course," I responded immediately and was impressed with how quickly my cock was back in action at the mere thought of the two of them together.

"Okay, what about oral or fucking?"

"Yes and yes," I groaned.

"And I would say that I'm okay with those things too, for you. And if anything happens while I'm not around, I'm also okay with that. I just want to know all the salacious details afterward."

Bracing my hand on the shower wall in front of me, I let the steaming water run over my head as I turned to look at her. She had a coy little smile tilting her lips, but it was all a ruse. She was so fucking dirty.

"Fuck, sweet girl. Are you trying to go for round two before dinner?"

"Nope," she said, popping the *p*. "We are simply discussing boundaries and limits. What if we went on dates separately?"

"I'd probably feel a little left out, but I'm sure it's important. If it's going to work at all, we're going to need to establish our own separate relationships and make sure those are strong."

"I'm impressed," she said, and my chest welled with pride. "You're so right."

Palmer was much more knowledgeable about these things. Her parents had been in a polyamorous relationship many years ago and didn't keep it a secret. They were open about their experiences and that, although they truly loved the woman they had been with, it hadn't worked out for all the normal reasons relationships don't often work.

"Wait. So why didn't your kiss in high school go anywhere? Nothing happened after that, right?"

I shook my head and shivered with the lingering endorphins from my orgasm.

"It was kind of a mixture of things, but ultimately, we were never single at the same time. Either he was dating someone, or I was. Hell, when we kissed, he was with a girl. It was really shitty on my part, but we were young and stupid."

"That makes sense. Well, I think that's good for now," Palmer said. "And if anything goes awry or you don't like something, we always have our safe word."

"Fucking lasagna," I supplied, and she giggled like usual.

five

. . .

Liam

SITTING at our table in the fancy restaurant, I swirled the expensive tequila I'd splurged on and waited for Palmer and Easton.

I felt out of place wearing a sports coat and sipping liquor that cost almost double what I would normally pay for a bottle, but what the hell. When in Colorado and newly single while third wheeling on a trip with your best friends, what else was there to do?

I'd taken the longest shower I could, enjoying the warm water and the rainfall showerhead while trying to get my thoughts in order.

Then I'd looked up the restaurant and realized the dress code required that men wear jackets or sports coats. I only had one, so I tossed it on over my button-up shirt before I headed out of my room. Thankfully, there wasn't a rule against jeans because that's all I'd packed.

I expected Palmer and Easton to beat me there, but ten minutes later, they were officially late. Completely out of character for both of them, my anxiety climbed until I looked up just in time to spot the two of them. My nerves burned away, leaving captivation in their wake. I saw Easton first, as he led Palmer through the dining room.

He was dressed in a perfectly tailored dark blue suit and white button-down shirt. His black hair was styled and combed to the side, and he'd trimmed his short beard to show off his square jawline.

That little spark of attraction that I always carried with me—the one I intently kept locked down—engulfed me. The inferno felt like it would burn me alive when he stepped to the side, and I caught my first glimpse of Palmer.

They'd both gotten even more attractive with every year that passed.

Since the restaurant was in the same building as our rooms, she didn't have a jacket or coat to cover up the absolutely jaw-dropping dress. My mouth went dry, and I had willed my cock to behave before I stood to greet them.

It was a satin sheath number that bunched at her curves and was low enough to give a teasing peek at her cleavage. It was a shade of green that matched Easton's eyes.

"Damn, Liam," Palmer drawled. She reached for me first and wrapped an arm around my neck. Her breasts pressed against me, and I fought a groan. "You clean up nice."

She pulled back, and I was impressed with the dark shadow rimming her eyes that made the deep brown pop.

"You, too, Sparky," I said, but the words were much deeper than usual. A little bit of that lust slipped through, and Palmer's eyes shot to mine, intrigue pooling behind them like she'd heard it too.

But if she had, she kept that knowledge to herself and stepped aside for her husband.

Easton gave me a hug, nothing out of the ordinary there, but the way he lingered made me begin to question if something else was going on. I hugged him back and made the mistake of sucking in a deep breath. All I was hit with was the smell of *him.*

I pulled away quickly and plopped down in my chair, hoping he couldn't feel my rapidly hardening cock.

Palmer had taken the seat next to me. I expected Easton to take the one next to her at our table meant for four, but instead, he sat down next to me and across from his wife.

Our server appeared and took our drink orders before I could think any more about it. I ordered another tequila—I would worry about my wallet later—while Palmer ordered a whiskey and Easton asked for some gin-based drink he liked.

The waiter disappeared, and Palmer dropped her elbows onto the table. Whether she meant to or not, the move pushed her tits together and gave both Easton and me a very nice view down her dress—the dress that apparently didn't require a bra.

"So you're sure you're okay?" she asked.

Clearing my throat, I ran my finger around the rim of my empty glass.

"Yeah, I'm fine. Being dumped isn't fun, but like I said, it's for the best."

Palmer nodded and looked across the table at Easton. A silent conversation passed between them, and not for the first time did I feel a twinge of jealousy at their connection.

"So did you get that new project?" I asked Easton, hoping to move the conversation past my breakup.

Our waiter dropped our drinks off, and we quickly agreed on a few different appetizers. "Actually, I got the call when we landed," Easton said with a smile. "They want me to design all their new law offices. We're going to nail down the details when we're back."

"Holy shit." I lifted my glass, and my best friend followed my lead, tapping them together. "I'm so fucking proud of you, but I never doubted that you'd get it."

Easton took a sip of his drink and sighed as he set it back down on the table. Looking between Palmer and me, he settled back in his chair. "The two of you have been my biggest cheerleaders. I wouldn't have accomplished half of what I have if it weren't for you."

Easton was a great friend, and he was always the first to tell me how important our friendship was and how much he appreciated it. But my heart always skipped a beat when he did.

"And we wouldn't have it any other way," Palmer added. Without looking at her, I could hear the smile in her voice. Since my attention was averted, I hadn't noticed her reach for me, so I startled when her hand landed on top of mine.

I peered down at our hands first, making sure I wasn't hallucinating, and when I confirmed that wasn't the case, I gazed up at her. There was a soft, kind smile sitting on her pink-painted lips.

While I was in my own head trying to determine why she wasn't letting go, Palmer and Easton continued discussing his upcoming project. She didn't let go for several minutes, and I had to pay extremely close attention to the conversation so I knew when to pop in at the right time.

She didn't release my hand until our appetizers arrived, and it felt like she did so reluctantly. The way she slid her fingers against my palm made goosebumps appear across my skin.

The rest of our dinner was more or less normal. We discussed the two new apprentices I hired, and Palmer was beginning a huge marketing campaign at work. She was also struggling, along with her mother, to keep her father on his doctor-prescribed diet. If he wanted to prevent another heart attack, he had to eat in a very specific way.

On the surface, they both appeared normal, but I could sense something was different. The way Palmer kept touching my arm, and Easton made a show of resting his arm on the back of my chair and sliding his legs wider so our knees would touch.

I might not have been privy to their little silent conversations and couple sorcery, but we'd been friends long enough that I knew something was up.

six

. . .

Liam

AFTER A FILLING MEAL, drinks, and dessert that Palmer insisted on, we all three stumbled off the elevator happy and almost crying with laughter.

Easton was telling us about the woman sitting next to him on the plane and the god-awful smell coming from the child she was holding. The way he described it had both Palmer and me fighting for our lives and wiping tears from our eyes.

By the time we'd composed ourselves, we were at our respective doors.

I straightened and fished my key card out of my pocket.

"Dinner was so good. You said tomorrow is our spa day, right? What time do we have to be there?"

"I booked us all massages at ten, but…" Palmer trailed off and looked up at her husband, who had his arm slung over her shoulders. Fuck, they looked so good together.

Another silent conversation, and Easton looked back at me.

"Want a nightcap?" he asked, tilting his head toward their door. "I bought a tequila I think you'll enjoy."

What would one more drink hurt? And he knew my weakness.

I nodded, and Palmer excitedly let us into their room. She pushed open the door and looked back just a few steps in, like she was making sure we were both following.

"Every so often, she does something like that," Easton said. He closed the door behind us and gazed lovingly at Palmer, who was kicking off her heels and plopping down on the bed. "And it reminds me exactly why you call her Sparky."

I smiled at the memory of the first time I'd called her Sparky. Besides Easton calling her P, apparently, she'd never had a nickname, and she'd lit up the first time I'd said it. I was trying to make her light up the same way ever since.

Easton shrugged off his jacket, and I followed his lead, dropping mine down on the same chair. Palmer appeared in front of me with a glass that had a few ice cubes and a healthy pour of amber-colored tequila. I smelled it first and tried to place it as I took the first sip.

Instantly, I knew it was the same tequila I'd been drinking at dinner.

Lowering my glass, I glanced between them. "This is what I was drinking at dinner," I said. "Is that just a coincidence, or..." My words trailed off, and my answer first came from Palmer's wide, gleeful smile, then by way of Easton.

"I had them bring a bottle up here when I noticed how much you liked it." He said it casually while he unbuttoned his shirt sleeves and rolled them up his forearms. He didn't even look at me when he poured himself a glass and took a generous sip.

Neither of them acted like it was a big deal, but the bottle wasn't bottom shelf. It cost more than a pretty penny and was a really thoughtful gesture.

Across the room, Palmer found her phone and connected it to the TV. She started playing rock music that we all enjoyed and plopped down on the bed. She unclipped her hair and let her dark brown strands fall free. Still in her green dress but shoeless and relaxed, she was utterly breathtaking.

"Sit," she instructed me, pointing to one of the two chairs positioned by the window. Their view was the same, and I took a moment to take in the wonder of the snow and lights before I sat. It was a large leather chair that even my six-foot-two, well over two-hundred-pound self had extra room in.

Easton took the other chair and set his tequila on the table between us.

"This place is amazing," I murmured. I could still see the snow falling out the window over Easton's shoulder, and it was mesmerizing to watch.

My mom had raised me by herself and worked three jobs to even keep food on the table. When we'd moved into the house next door to Easton, it had been as the help. My mom was a live-in housekeeper and cook for the family that lived there.

She did her best, but we couldn't afford vacations like these. After she died my freshman year of college, I realized it didn't matter. She was the best mom I could have asked for, and now I worked my ass off to take trips like this for both of us.

I knew she would have loved it here.

"It really is," Palmer sighed. "Someone posted about it on social media, and when Easton showed me, I knew we had to take a trip. It's just so beautiful and peaceful."

"And dinner was damn good. I could have had three more bowls of pasta," Easton added.

"Your steak looked really good too," I told Palmer, and she nodded emphatically.

"It was amazing. We'll have to go back before we leave. We can order a few things and share each dish."

"Good idea, Sparky."

Her smile made my chest tighten, and she sat up, stretching her arms out to her sides and glancing quickly at Easton.

"How's your tequila, Liam?"

She asked just as I was taking a long sip. I savored the way the cool liquor burned my throat as it slid down and settled warmly in my stomach.

"So good. I know you don't usually like tequila, but you should try it. You've got a whole bottle."

Looking over her shoulder, she eyed the bottle still sitting on their dresser and then looked at Easton's half-full glass. But her eyes landed back on me and the drink in my hand.

"I should try it," she said. In one graceful motion, she slid off the bed and didn't bother to straighten her dress that had hiked around her thighs. She took one step, then another, and by the time she lifted her leg again, I realized she wasn't walking toward her husband but toward me.

I tensed, one hand gripping the arm of the chair and the other holding the glass so tightly I worried it might shatter. Suddenly, she was standing in front of me, the front of her thighs brushing my knees. I could feel the way she looked at me through my entire body, like every nerve was raw, and I was propelled by need alone.

She stopped for the briefest second, long enough for me to suck in a breath I desperately needed, then she was moving again. She pulled her dress up even higher and planted one knee on the chair beside my leg. The other leg followed, and Palmer was suddenly straddling my lap.

I was breathing hard and doing my damndest to keep my shit together, but when her hands fell against my chest, I nearly came undone.

Thankfully, she gave me a moment to comprehend what was happening and didn't immediately sit directly down on my throbbing erection that was poised beneath her. But I could feel her heat and was captivated by the lust shining bright in her eyes.

This couldn't be happening. Fuck, I hoped it was happening, but I couldn't believe it.

My eyes ate up the sight of her on top of me—the curve of her hips and the way her thighs spread around my legs. I eyed the smallest part of her waist and wanted to feel how well my hands would fit there. Higher yet, my gaze climbed, and her lack of a bra was more noticeable than before. Her nipples were hard and straining against the satin, the perfect outline that I imagined sucking and biting through the fabric.

Hell, even her collarbone was perfect, and when my attention settled on her face again, she licked her lips and stared down at my mouth.

"I want to try it," she said, and my mind reeled. The tequila —she was talking about the tequila. "But not from the bottle or a glass."

My brain was incapable of thought as she cupped my face and leaned forward.

Her mouth was soft yet confident against mine, and she slipped her tongue over my lips, requesting entry that I was eager to grant. Our tongues brushed, and she moaned at the first touch.

It was just enough for her to taste the remnants of tequila and leave me wanting so much more.

She leaned back and licked her lips, closing her eyes like she was savoring the flavor.

"It is *so* good," she said. "I think I need more."

My hand was unrelenting against the arm of the chair as I tried my best not to touch her. When she leaned forward again, I suddenly became more than aware of Easton just a chair away.

Guilt washed over me, but I hadn't been the one to initiate the kiss.

Easton's expression was passive. He stared back at me and casually took a swig of his drink. One ankle crossed over his other knee, he was leaned back in the chair like this was nothing out of the ordinary, all while my heart felt like it was going to beat out of my chest. They'd have to take me to the hospital if it kept up that way.

While I was trying to judge Easton's feelings on what was happening right in front of him, Palmer kissed my stubble-covered jaw, then neck, and behind my ear. She pressed sensual, open-mouth kisses everywhere she could reach.

All I wanted to do was press up against her, feel the heat between her legs against my aching cock, and try to sate the fire that was burning me alive.

Tilting back, she caught Easton and me in a stare down. He was winning, though, his expression unchanging.

"Are you looking at him for permission?" she asked, tiptoeing her fingers up my throat until she reached my mouth and pulled my bottom lip down. She swiped across it and stared like she wanted more. "Do you like being told what to do in the bedroom?"

I growled at her words, which had obviously been her intent, to stir me into action and push me further. And I wasn't anywhere near strong enough to resist, even if I wanted to.

"Not usually, but if you kiss me again, Sparky, I'm not going to be able to stop. So I figured I should talk to *your husband* before I touch his wife."

Palmer's jaw dropped, and she looked over at Easton. I followed her line of sight, and finally, *finally* saw a change in his expression. One side of his mouth ticked up in the smallest smile.

He looked directly at me, green eyes burning bright, and nodded.

That was all the permission I needed. In one swift motion, I set my glass on the table between our chairs and reached for Palmer. One hand cupped her cheek, the other wrapped around her back. She dropped on top of me, and we both groaned into our fierce kiss.

There was nothing chaste or sweet about our second—actually third—kiss. There wasn't any of the shame or guilt that marred our first kiss, or the lingering sadness and tears on her lips when we were in the hospital waiting room, hoping for good news about her dad.

This one was all desire and longing.

My hands slipped over the smooth satin of her dress, and my fingers tangled in her soft hair as I pressed her closer. Her lips were urgent yet pliable against mine, and I craved the way she let me lead the kiss.

Our tongues tangled, and her nails scraped against my neck as she gripped my hair. I was enthralled by every little sound she made, the vibration of which I felt against my mouth, and the urgent roll of her hips against my cock.

Even with the fabric between us, I felt like I was seconds from coming, and I nearly lost control when Easton murmured in a low voice, "Make her come, Liam. Make my wife come."

seven

. . .

Palmer

My plan wasn't exactly a plan. My plan was just to see where the night went and wait for my opening.

And when he offered me a taste of the tequila, I saw my opportunity.

With his hands on me and his lips against mine, I felt like I was flying. Easton's eyes on us only heightened every sensation and movement.

Liam was different from Easton, and I wouldn't have wanted them to be the same, no matter how much I liked being with both of them. Liam was broad, and I could feel his dense, muscular chest beneath my hands. He also had blond hair that brushed his shoulders and was fun to grip and pull. Especially since it made him groan into my mouth and his cock twitch beneath me.

A cock I was eager to get to know better, but that my pussy was already getting acquainted with. One of his large hands twisted in my hair, guiding our kiss and exploring my mouth, while the other splayed around my waist and urged me to move faster over him.

"Make her come, Liam. Make my wife come." Easton's voice was a low, guttural command.

"Oh, fuck," I muttered against Liam's lips, breaking apart for the first time so we could both look in Easton's direction.

He was staring at us with barely restrained lust simmering behind his green eyes, but was seated so casually in his leather chair, one ankle crossed over his opposite knee. His erection was thick and noticeable, straining against the dark blue fabric, and I licked my lips.

He was so fucking hot.

His glass of tequila was still half full, and he traced a finger around the rim as he watched us from under hooded eyes.

"Do you like that idea, sweet girl?" he asked, and I nodded. I could feel Liam's warm breath on my cheek as he watched me. Knowing him, he was gauging my reactions to make sure I was all in.

But I wouldn't be sitting on his lap unless I was.

Liam's hands tightened on me, pulling my hair just enough that I gasped. His other hand massaged my hip. His fingers were splayed against my ass, but I wanted them everywhere all at once.

"Then do it. Show Liam how pretty you are when you come."

Liam kissed my neck, and I moaned at the pressure of his lips.

"Do you wanna come for me, Palmer?"

I whimpered and jerked my hips in response. "Please. I want to come for you. For both of you."

His smile was all devious intent, and I loved that I was on the receiving end of it.

"Lean back, sweet girl. Show me your pretty pussy." After one last lingering kiss on my lips, he collared his hand around my throat but kept me steady with his other on my hip.

And I did as he asked. I leaned back and braced my hands on his knees behind me, giving him easy access to between my legs.

My eyes flashed to Easton for a moment, and he caught my look. We both knew what he would find.

Liam removed his hand from my throat and slowly pushed the fabric of my dress up my hips. His rough, calloused fingers brushed against my thighs, and I shivered at the careful touch of such a large man.

He watched my face as he pooled the fabric around my hips, not glancing down until it was completely out of the way.

"Fuuuck," he groaned. He dropped his head back for a second and sucked in a deep breath. "You haven't been wearing panties all night?"

I shook my head, and Liam looked at Easton. "Did you know about this?"

Easton's mouth hitched in a crooked smile, and he nodded once. "I did. She's a dirty girl."

"Mmm," Liam hummed. His hands squeezed my hips as he looked back down at my mostly bare cunt. There was a neat triangle of hair just above my pubic bone, but everything else was gone.

"Such a dirty fucking girl," Liam murmured. His fingers splayed, and his thumbs teased the sensitive skin next to my pussy, so close to touching, but not close enough. "Good thing I love dirty. You were planning this, weren't you?"

"Yes," I hissed, both answering his question and verbalizing my excitement to feel his finger finally brush against my slit. My nails dug into the fabric of his jeans, and I bucked my hips up to meet his touch.

My body was a ball of tension, desire twisting and tightening every muscle. I was on the verge of combusting when I felt his thumbs spread me wide. Under heavy-lidded eyes, I looked down my body to see Liam staring at my cunt.

He licked his lips and flashed me a filthy smile.

I gasped at the first touch. His thumb massaged my clit, and I wanted to scream with ecstasy. Screwing my eyes shut, I saw sparks of light behind my lids as his fingers moved lower.

"So swollen and wet already," he said. "Such a gorgeous cunt. I bet it takes cock so well."

I tried to nod my head, but I was too blissed out to do much besides balance myself on his legs.

My entire body clenched when he speared two thick fingers inside me. There was a minor ache, but I liked the pain, and my body was nearly ready anyway. He wasn't kidding—I was wet, nearly dripping for him.

"Taste her," Easton instructed.

God, had his voice gotten even deeper?

I opened my eyes just long enough to watch Liam slip his fingers free and look directly at Easton as he sucked my pleasure off. At the view, Easton finally reacted, dropping his head back on the chair behind him and rubbing a hand over his erection.

But Liam didn't leave me wanting for long. He turned back and replaced his fingers inside me, easily reaching his thumb up to press against my clit.

Already on the precipice of an intense orgasm, he hooked his fingers inside me and immediately found my G-spot.

"Oh, fuck," I moaned. He drew pleasure from my body with ease, like we'd been doing this forever, and he knew how to get me there. Like Easton.

Thick fingers pumped into me, and he drew tight little circles over my clit. My hips moved of their own accord, riding his fingers and doing my best not to fall backward.

Realizing the precarious position I was in, Liam growled, "Come here."

He released my hip and grasped the back of my neck, tugging me forward while keeping me impaled on his fingers.

"Ride my fingers like you would my cock. Show me what this pussy can do."

I silently thanked the universe that Liam was a dirty talker too. Easton did unbelievable things with his dirty words, but having two of them? I was in for it.

Wrapping my arms around his neck, I dropped my forehead

to Liam's as I began to ride his fingers. I rolled my hips and fucked myself up and down, back and forth until I found that perfect rhythm that made my eyes roll back.

He took my lips in a bruising kiss, tongue demanding entry and claiming every sound I made.

Only seconds passed before I detonated. I cried out in blinding pleasure while Liam held me steadfast against him. He cursed under his breath, and I clamped around his fingers so tightly I worried I'd break them.

It took me a while to come down from my high, aftershocks whipping through my body. When I finally did, I sat back with a sated smile.

"Oh my god," I sighed. "Did I break your fingers?"

Liam chuckled and pulled the fingers in question free. I hated how empty I felt, but was slightly in awe of his perfectly intact fingers as he held them up. My orgasm coated them, and he licked them clean once again.

"That was incredible, Sparky."

"My beautiful girl, you should return the favor," Easton said, and I smiled over at my husband, whose chest was rising and falling quickly.

I kissed Liam, tasting my release on his tongue, then slid off his legs, making myself comfortable on my knees in front of him.

eight

. . .

Easton

I TOSSED the pillow I'd removed from the chair toward Palmer, who positioned it under her knees. She ran her palms up Liam's firm, strong thighs and played with the edge of his belt.

Seeing them together like this was incredible.

When Palmer stood and strode over to Liam earlier, a flash of panic whipped through me, like maybe I wouldn't be able to go through with it after all. But that feeling quickly faded and was replaced with a deep-seated lust and desire. They both looked over at me often, making sure I was watching and checking in that I was enjoying the view.

I'd never considered myself a voyeur, but watching the two of them together made my cock throb.

Liam dropped his head back against the chair and rolled it to the side to look at me.

"You have such a good wife," he said, and my chest inflated with pride.

"I do," I agreed with a small smile. Palmer tossed her hair behind her shoulders and cut her eyes at me. She was having so much fun. "Just wait until you feel her mouth. She sucks cock so well."

Liam's hazel eyes shuddered, and I ran the heel of my hand over my aching erection. I couldn't help it when I was watching Palmer unfasten Liam's belt and unzip his jeans.

"Take yourself out." My eyes flashed to Liam's in surprise. I wasn't sure if participating this first time around would be the best idea, but since it was Liam's idea, who the hell was I to say no? I was keen on making sure Palmer was comfortable and that she and Liam were comfortable together. If that meant I took a back seat, I was more than okay with that.

Dropping my hands to my belt, I yanked it open and lowered the zipper as Palmer helped Liam do the same. He lifted his hips, and Palmer tugged his jeans down low enough to expose his black briefs that were tight across his erection.

She leaned forward and kissed his shaft, then ran her tongue across the fabric and sucked his head through it. He moaned and bucked up into her mouth, his hands grabbing the armrests and looking down at her like he was in awe of the woman at his feet.

He should be. I was in awe of her too.

Tension swirled around us, and I held my breath as Palmer slid her fingers beneath his briefs and dragged them lower. His cock sprang free, and my mouth watered.

He was long and thick. A prominent vein ran up the side of his shaft, and precum was collecting at his tip. Palmer did exactly what I was thinking and leaned forward, suctioning her lips around his head.

Liam cursed, and I couldn't take it anymore. I pushed my briefs—the same ones as Liam's but in a dark blue—down my legs and freed my erection.

Wrapping a hand around my cock, I gazed at Palmer and Liam. Her hand looked small, fisted around the base of his dick, and she lowered her mouth down over him again and again, taking him deeper every time.

"You have such a pretty cock," I mused as I gripped mine. In our fifteen years of friendship, I'd seen Liam's dick a time or two. Not intentionally, but it's happened. I'd just never had the chance to really look at him, and now I might become a little obsessed.

With his jaw slack, Liam ran his fingers through her hair and fisted it at the back of her head. He held it out of the way as she bobbed on his cock.

When he looked over at me, his eyes dropped to my hand and where it was fisted. His eyelids dropped even lower, and I enjoyed the intensity of his attention.

I stroked myself in time to Palmer's movements over Liam. I didn't know where to look. There were too many good things happening in front of me—Palmer's bobbing at a glorious pace, and Liam's cock disappearing down her throat. Liam's face twisted in pleasure and desire.

I watched them and imagined that it wasn't my hand around my dick but Palmer's mouth—or Liam's—and I could feel the orgasm threatening. My balls were heavy, and I squeezed the tip harder to give myself a few extra seconds.

Thankfully, though, ecstasy washed across Liam's face. His orgasm barreled through him as his eyes were fixed on me.

"Fuck, fuck, *fuck,*" he chanted. He pistoned wildly into Palmer's waiting mouth, and I growled.

"Don't pull out, and P, you better not fucking swallow," I commanded. Although she couldn't acknowledge me with her mouth stuffed full of cock, I could tell by the flutter of her lids that she heard me.

In a second, I stood and walked the few feet to them. Palmer popped off Liam at the perfect time, and I replaced his hand in her hair with my own. Tugging her head back, she craned her neck and stuck out her tongue.

Fuck, she was perfect, knowing exactly what I wanted before I even had to ask.

Liam's cum was thick and white, and the sight made my orgasm bear down on me. My leg brushed Liam's, and his presence next to me was another heady reminder of what I'd just witnessed. I could hear his panted breaths and low curses as Palmer kept her mouth wide, and I shot against her tongue.

My hand shuttled up and down my shaft, and I had to force my eyes to stay open. My release hit her tongue and mixed with Liam's. I groaned and panted. The orgasm hit me so hard I didn't know if I would be able to stay standing without Liam's leg there to keep me upright.

Struggling to suck in a deep enough breath, I stepped back just enough for Liam to see what we'd done.

"Show him, sweet girl." With my fingers still tangled in her hair, Palmer turned her head and showed Liam the mixture of our release on her tongue. Spit ran down her chin, and her makeup was smeared from the face-fucking she took, but I didn't know if she'd ever looked more beautiful.

Liam leaned forward and gripped her throat with one massive hand.

"Swallow," we both said in unison. Liam flashed a quick, sated smile in my direction before we both watched Palmer disappear our release.

I released my hold on her head and ran my fingers gently through her tangled strands. "You're fucking beautiful," I murmured, and Palmer preened under the praise. Leaning down, I kissed her softly at first, but when I tasted us on her tongue, I couldn't help but deepen the kiss, spearing my tongue against hers and enjoying the flavor.

When we parted, Liam and I both helped Palmer stand on unsteady legs. Her knees were red, even with the pillow beneath her, but she was smiling.

She didn't hesitate to lean forward and kiss Liam too. It was the tender kiss of friends who had just become lovers, and I felt the tug of desire to be a part of it.

But we'd already pushed well past our friendship for one night.

Palmer leaned back and glanced at me over her shoulder before looking back at Liam.

"Will you stay with us tonight?"

Her question was quiet and sweet. Liam's eyes immediately flashed to mine, and I ran a hand down Palmer's back.

"You should," I agreed, and Liam nodded.

"Think the bed is big enough for the three of us?" he asked, and we all considered the king-sized bed behind us.

Palmer smiled. "We may have to cuddle, but I think we can make do."

nine

. . .

Liam

PALMER STRETCHED NEXT to me and snuggled closer into my bare chest.

I opened my eyes just enough to glance at the clock across the room. Just after nine in the morning, which meant if we didn't get up soon, we were going to be late for our massages. Although staying in bed with the two of them all day didn't sound like such a bad idea.

After a day of traveling and completely altering our friendships forever, we were all exhausted, so there wasn't much preamble or discussion before we fell into bed. Palmer curled up between us, resting her head on me as Easton curled around her from behind.

I was out seconds later and slept more peacefully than I could remember.

Palmer was sleeping soundly against me, and she was beautiful with her hair fanned out wildly around her and a sleepy smile resting on her lips. I kissed her forehead and caught Easton watching us.

"Morning," he whispered, and I loved how sleep made his voice gruff and deeper.

"Morning," I whispered back.

"How do you feel?"

He didn't clarify his question further, but I knew what he meant. He wanted to know if I regretted it. Honestly, I'd expected there to be some weirdness. It wouldn't be strange to feel a little awkwardness or confusion when waking up with both of them.

But I didn't. I quickly took a poll of my feelings, combing through every thought and emotion, and I couldn't come up with anything that felt even close to regret.

It felt good to have them both so close. I wasn't sure what had changed between when they'd greeted me in my room and dinner, but something had.

And I planned to figure out what exactly it was today, but I wasn't going to question the outcome.

"Good," I said. "Really good."

I hadn't realized Palmer was also awake until she mumbled a sleepy little, "Me too," against my chest. Her eyes fluttered open and squinted up at me.

"Good morning, beautiful," Easton said, rolling over and kissing Palmer on the neck.

"This is really nice, but if we don't get up now, we're going to be late for our massage appointments."

Palmer groaned and buried her face against my neck, slinging her arm around my shoulder. "But more sleep sounds so good."

I chuckled and smoothed a hand over her back. "You can sleep during your massage, Sparky."

"And we can always get back in bed afterward," Easton said. He reached for Palmer, and the back of his hand brushed against me as he wrapped it around her stomach. My muscles clenched, and my skin felt warm under his brief touch.

Easton didn't notice my reaction as Palmer rolled into his

embrace with another groan. She had tossed on one of Easton's T-shirts before we'd crawled into bed, but she smelled like me too.

"Promise?" Palmer asked. When Easton nodded and kissed her, she looked back at me, waiting for a response.

"I could never deny you."

Her smile was bright, and her kiss was hungry. She fisted her hands in my hair and pressed herself against me. I couldn't hold in my groan.

"This is not helping anyone. Let's go." Easton rolled out of bed and dragged Palmer with him. I flipped back the covers and was immediately accosted by the cold air.

Pausing for a moment, I realized I had to go back to my room to get dressed, and that I had to leave them both in their room. It was the first time in at least several hours that I'd been confronted with the fact that they're a couple, and I'm... not.

Staring at the door leading to my bedroom, Palmer came up behind me and wrapped her arms around my stomach. She kissed my back and hummed against my skin.

"See you in a few minutes?"

I covered her hands with one of mine and didn't know if I'd ever get used to these little displays of affection.

"Yeah, a few minutes," I agreed, and I could feel her smile.

"And then maybe we can talk about you staying in our room the rest of the time?"

Pleasantly surprised, my heart collided with the inside of my chest, and I wanted to pump my fist in the air.

"Something we can discuss," I said instead, and she placed one last kiss on my back before she strutted away, Easton's T-shirt riding up and showing the rounded curve of her ass.

Twenty minutes later, we were all climbing into the elevator. When the doors closed, I asked the burning question that had been on my mind.

"So what happened? What changed?"

They looked at each other, and Palmer wrapped her tan coat tighter around her.

"Well," she began. "We just…we—"

"We realized there might be something more here," Easton finished for her. "And we weren't really keen on waiting to explore it. Then you were on the receiving end of Palmer's plan to see if you felt the same."

"Hey, I think it worked," she defended, smacking her hand playfully against Easton's stomach.

I crossed my arms over my chest and leaned back against the elevator wall, chuckling softly at their antics. "It did work," I agreed. "I don't know in what world it wouldn't have. But what prompted it? This is just…I never expected it."

"I guess your breakup kind of did," Palmer said. "We both realized that all we want is for you to be happy, and we thought that maybe…*we* could make you happy. That we wanted to be the ones to make you happy."

No words felt like enough response, so I did the second-best thing. I closed the distance between us, not that there was much in the small elevator, and cradled her face in my hands as I slanted my mouth over hers. The elevator ride wasn't long enough for it to go much further, but it was enough to show her just how much I appreciated their realization and how thankful I was that they'd had it. Because as much as I wanted them too, I wouldn't have made the first move. They were already in a committed relationship, and I wouldn't be the one to fuck that up.

But if they wanted me. If they *both* wanted me, I was all in.

The elevator stopped, and I looked up to see Easton smiling at us. His hands were stuffed into his coat pockets, and I knew I wanted to kiss him too. I just didn't know if he wanted the same.

We made the short walk to the spa building and hurried inside and out of the cold. The interior of the spa was warm and relaxing—exactly what a spa should be.

"Hi, guys. How can I help you?"

"We have a reservation under Winters," Easton said.

"Ahh, yes," the woman said, peering down at her computer. There were candles and lotions on the counter, and I surveyed the different scents while the lady clicked away on her keyboard. "I have a reservation for four, two couples' massages."

Reaching for a candle that apparently smelled like smoky vanilla, my hand froze midair.

"That's it, but there's actually just three of us now," Palmer said.

"Okay, no problem. I'll just put, umm…Palmer and Easton in their own room as planned, and Liam will be in a single room."

"Actually," Palmer interrupted. She squeezed past Easton and stepped up to the counter, drumming her fingertips on the dark wood surface. "Is it going to cause a problem if we switch things up?"

The lady cocked her head to the side but shrugged. "No, no problem. Would you like to change the rooms?"

"Yes!" Palmer exclaimed. "Easton and Liam would like to share one room, and I'll take the single one."

Easton and I looked at each other, then back at Palmer as the woman behind the counter confirmed that it wouldn't be a problem.

Palmer spun with her hands excitedly clasped together in front of her.

"Sweet girl, you are devious," Easton chided, but Palmer just shrugged.

"I know."

ten

. . .

Easton

"WE'RE GOING to go ahead and step out. Take your time getting dressed, and please take advantage of the sauna and hot tub, which are in the hallway on your left."

The massage therapists stepped out, but I didn't move until I heard the door click closed. I'd never been more relaxed, even though my mind couldn't stop thinking about Liam lying three feet away from me, mostly naked under his own sheet. When I'd flipped onto my back, I'd had to start thinking about anything and everything other than what we'd done last night. Thinking about Palmer's lips around his cock or how beautiful she was writhing over his fingers would have made for a really uncomfortable massage with my dick tenting the sheet.

Slowly, I sat up and swung my legs over the table as Liam did the same. His blond hair was mussed, and there was a relaxed smile sitting on his lips.

Lips I sincerely needed to feel on mine sooner rather than later.

"That was amazing," Liam said, rolling his shoulders and tilting his head to one side, then the other. My eyes scanned the broad plane of his chest, and the smattering of light brown hair in the center that led down to what I knew was an impressive dick.

"It was," I muttered. "Should we head to the locker room?"

He nodded, and we both stood. We dropped our sheets on each bed and grabbed the robes they'd provided. If we didn't get out of the room immediately, we weren't going to leave until he was on his knees, choking on my cock.

We stepped out into the hallway, and Liam followed just behind me as I found the door to the locker room, which contained the sauna, showers, and hot tub.

Everything was dark and moody, the tile a deep gray and warm under my feet. We slipped around the corner and surveyed the space. We were alone in the large room.

"Hot tub?" Liam asked. He motioned to the octagon-shaped pool at the back of the room. It sat beneath three large windows that looked out onto snow-covered trees.

I hung my robe on one of the hooks and turned around to see Liam already stepping into the steaming water. My mouth went dry as he sank lower and settled onto a seat.

For years, I'd been sure to keep any feelings that weren't strictly friend-like buried so deep down that there was never a chance they would accidentally slip to the surface. But now that I no longer had to keep them hidden, it was a little overwhelming. It was like I was feeling everything again for the first time.

"Winters?" I shook my head and realized I'd been staring at Liam for much longer than appropriate.

Suddenly, my cheeks were burning, and fuck, was I blushing?

"Sorry. I just, uh…zoned out," I muttered, stepping down into the hot tub and taking a seat on the step across from Liam.

His long, toned arms were stretched out across the edge behind him, showing off one of his few tattoos on his inner biceps—lyrics from one of his favorite songs written in his mom's handwriting.

"Thinking about last night?"

My eyes snapped to his, and his knowing smirk made my cock stir.

"And this morning," I said, returning his smirk with one of my own. I ran my hands over the top of the bubbling water and enjoyed the feel of the jets on my lower back.

"So Palmer has been pretty open about how she feels about… this. And I'm guessing you feel the same, but if that's not the case—"

"It is," I agreed quickly. "I want this. We both want this."

Liam nodded, but his eyes dropped to the water in front of him, and I could feel his unspoken thoughts.

"Talk to me," I said.

He dragged a wet hand through his blond hair and dropped his shoulders as he sighed. "I guess my question is, what is this? You say you both want *this,* but no one has explained what *this* is. Is it…" He glanced around, making sure we were still alone before he continued, "Is it just sex?"

"Never." For as tumultuous as my emotions were, my responses came easily. "It could never be just sex with you. That's just a really nice perk."

"Good to know," he said. He looked past me, out to the snow-covered landscape, and I knew that wasn't enough. He was in his head, and that's the last thing I wanted.

Taking a deep, grounding breath, I stood, which drew Liam's attention back to me. He watched me as I slowly walked through the waist-deep water to where he sat. I stopped directly in front of him, my legs brushing his knees, and he tilted his head back.

Before I did anything else, I took a moment just to look at him. I knew him so well, but I hadn't had the opportunity to memorize his face the way I wanted to—to openly study the shallow lines around his hazel eyes and the cut of his jaw, the way his stubble was a shade or two darker than his hair, and the slight scar just below his lower lip.

His prominent Adam's apple bobbed as he swallowed, and his solid shoulders rose ever so slightly with his next breath.

Taking another slow step, Liam opened his legs beneath the water and let me stand between them. He watched me with curious eyes, and I swore he could hear how hard my heart was pounding.

I lifted my hands out of the water and wrapped them around the sides of his neck. His eyes fluttered closed for a moment, and I ran my thumb over his cheek.

When his eyes opened once again, gone was any doubt, replaced by a stirring heat. Something settled in my chest, being able to openly touch him and feel him beneath my hands. It was something I'd only felt once before with Palmer.

I couldn't wait a second longer. I leaned down and pressed my lips to his. It was soft, tentative, yet powerful all the same. And it was better than I remembered.

Liam groaned, and I felt it everywhere. His hands grabbed my hips, and I returned his groan with one of my own when his blunt nails dug into my skin. He took the opportunity with my lips parted to slip his tongue against mine, and I rocked my hips forward, searching for some relief.

My hands tightened against his face, and I tilted his head to direct our kiss. But he fought for dominance, giving as good as he got. His scruff scraped against my short beard, and I reveled in the delicious yet new sensation. It had been a really long time since I'd kissed a man with facial hair. Actually, it'd been almost fifteen years.

A door banged open somewhere else in the room, and I immediately jerked back. Liam let me go too, and I put enough space between us that no one would assume anything was happening before.

Liam rolled his lips, and I ran my fingers over mine, enjoying the phantom feeling of him. A man in sweats walked through the room and stopped in front of a locker. He opened it, and I glanced back down at Liam, who was looking up at me from beneath hooded lids.

I stared at the man's back, silently willing him to hurry the fuck up so I could resume kissing my best friend. Nervous energy thrummed through me as the man slowly gathered his belongings and closed the locker.

He was staring down at his phone and leisurely strolling out of the room with no care in the world. The second I heard the door shut again, I was reaching for Liam's hand and dragging him out of the hot tub.

"What—where are we going?" he asked. I grabbed two towels from the rack around the corner and slipped into a shower stall that was halfway down the row. I closed the door behind us, flipped the water on to warm, and turned to push Liam up against the dark gray tiled wall.

He gasped at the impact, and I swallowed down the sound as I slammed my mouth down on his. My hands slipped back into his hair, gripping his blond locks and tugging him closer. He did the same with his hands pressed against my lower back, and both of us moaned as our cocks pressed together.

Liam pushed off the wall and led me backward until we were both positioned under the showerhead. Warm water cascaded over us, and Liam ground his cock against me.

"Oh, fuck," I moaned against his wet lips, and he did it again.

"Wait, wait," he said abruptly, pushing against my chest and putting space between us. "We can't."

My entire world turned upside down with those two words.

"Why not?"

"Palmer," he said. He dragged his hands through his soaked hair, then wiped them down his face. "How…how do we know if she's okay with this? You're married, Easton."

My terror subsided, and I took a step closer. He put a hand up to try to stop me, but I easily batted it away. He didn't put up much of a fight as I stepped into his space. I ran my hands down his chest and sucked in a deep, rumbling breath as my fingers slipped down his stomach.

I rested them just above the waistband of his briefs and eyed the thick outline of his erection.

"She's okay with it," I explained. "Before dinner last night, we discussed our limits, including if we were okay with either of us being alone with you. And we both unequivocally agreed that, yes, that's what we want. She reconfirmed it this morning, urging me to 'take advantage of any alone time we had together.'"

His hazel eyes were locked on mine as I rubbed my fingers along his waistband, closer to his cock. His breath hitched, and his head hit the wall behind him.

"Unless this is a limit for you, because I'm not going to make you—"

Do anything you don't want to, I was going to say, but didn't get a chance to. Liam flipped us around and kissed me hard.

eleven

. . .

Easton

Before I could catch my breath, Liam reached down the front of my briefs and wrapped his hot hand around me. One hand slammed against the tile behind him as my other gripped his hip, and I thrusted harder into his hand.

"I want this," he growled against my lips. "I want this more than I've ever wanted anything before."

"Fuck, yes. That's all I wanted to hear."

He squeezed the tip of my cock, and I speared my hand into his briefs. I moaned as my fingers wrapped around his thick shaft. I broke our kiss so I could see his eyes roll back, although I immediately missed his mouth. I wished there was a way I could keep kissing him and watch the ecstasy wash over his features.

"Yes, East, just like that," he chanted. He was hard and smooth in my hand, but our briefs were hindering the view. Tugging them down, we both glanced between us and were greeted with a perfect fucking sight.

His calloused palm stroked up and down my slightly longer, darker cock, while my fingers stretched around his thick length in even strokes.

All the pent-up arousal and desire was too much to hold off.

"I'm going to come in your hand," I panted. "Come with me. Come with—" My words broke off in a guttural groan which echoed through the quiet locker room. That was until Liam had the wherewithal to slam his lips over mine and swallow the sound as I pumped into his hand.

A second later, he moaned and gripped the back of my neck as I felt his body tighten against mine and his cum pulsed into my hand. When we'd finally both come down from our twin highs, I dropped my forehead to his and looked down at the mess we'd made.

We were both covered in each other's release, and I hummed with satisfaction.

"You both have made me come more than I thought possible," he murmured, not yet releasing my dick.

"Happy to help," I quipped as I lifted my hand and licked the remnants of him from each of my fingers. He watched me with a hungry gaze and followed my lead, licking me from his hand too.

We stumbled back under the water, hands exploring each other as we kissed and laughed. By the time we were dressed and heading back out to the hallway where we promised to meet Palmer, we were both lighter on our feet.

Our hands intertwined, we spotted Palmer in a large chair that appeared even larger, cradling her petite frame. She was gazing at her phone next to a floor-to-ceiling window that looked out onto another snowy landscape. The way her eyes skipped over the screen, I knew she was reading.

She didn't spot us until we were a few feet away, but when she did, her face lit up with the most perfect smile. Her brown eyes dropped to our joined hands and then flashed to our smiling faces as they twinkled with interest.

"You two look much more relaxed than you did two hours ago," she said in a knowing voice. She pocketed her phone and stood.

Liam took a deep breath and looked over at me. I loved the easy smile that tilted his lips—so unbidden and effortless.

"The massage was great," he said, then added a little quieter, "But what we just did in the shower helped so much more."

Palmer groaned, and we both reached for her at the same time. She stepped into our hold, and Liam kissed her first. Then she turned and gave me a similar lingering kiss.

"You'll have to tell me about it. I want every detail."

twelve

. . .

Palmer

RELAXED FROM OUR MASSAGES, we headed back to our rooms and changed. The cold wind was rough on my face and made my eyes incessantly water, so I didn't bother putting on any makeup. Instead, I ran a brush through my hair and put on another layer of moisturizer before I bundled up in my thickest clothes.

I hated being cold.

When I stepped out of the bathroom and into our room, Easton was lugging Liam's belongings through the adjoining door. He tossed them down beside our suitcases, and I plopped down on the bed to tug on my boots.

East gave me a quick kiss on the forehead and took his turn in the bathroom. When he disappeared, Liam popped his head around the door and glanced around the room.

"He took my stuff, didn't he?"

With a smile, I nodded and pointed at his open suitcase and duffel bag.

Liam chuckled and headed toward his stuff. He stopped too, though, and kissed me exactly where Easton had. The amount of love pulsing through me made me lightheaded. And hell, if I were dizzy for the rest of my life, I wouldn't be upset.

Liam and I walked hand-in-hand as we approached a cute little boutique on the resort property. Liam opened the door for me, but before stepping inside, we both looked back at Easton. He was locked in a conversation with a few random guests we'd met two seconds earlier.

Liam and I politely excused ourselves to get out of the cold, but Easton had stayed behind. They were also out shopping before their dinner reservations later.

"Always so outgoing," Liam mumbled, and I smiled back at Easton. He was the most outgoing of the three of us. He always had been and likely always would be. He was so personable, and everyone loved him.

"I know. But we love him for it."

At that, he waved goodbye to the small group and jogged over to us, his breath coming out in white puffs around his head.

"They invited us to dinner tonight, but I told them we already had plans." Liam and I shook our heads as we headed inside.

The warm air felt amazing on my chilled skin. I pulled off my gloves and unraveled my scarf before I got too hot.

It was a cute little boutique with jewelry, gifts, and clothes—one of those stores I would spend hours in if I could, looking at each of the one-of-a-kind items and spending way too much damn money.

After we left our room, we'd explored the resort grounds, walking into little shops and playing in the snow we didn't often see in Texas.

It had been one of my favorite days, and it was exactly the day we needed. It proved that the three of us together were as easy as breathing.

The little boutique we'd found ourselves in would likely be our last stop. We were all starving and cold.

"What do you think about this?" Liam asked as I was sifting through handmade earrings, trying to find a pair that called to me. He lifted up a blue sweater dress that looked exceptionally cozy and very cute.

"For you?" I asked coyly. "You do look great in blue."

He shook his head at my antics, and I caught Easton's smile as he looked at a wall of Lodge-branded gifts and souvenirs.

"Although I don't doubt I would look fucking fabulous in this dress, I think it would look even better on you."

He held it out to me, and I took it, running my hand over the soft fabric. Whether it looked amazing on or not, I knew I was going to buy it and wear it all the time. Especially around Liam, because I knew every time I did, it would make him smile. And Liam's smiles were too fucking special not to admire.

Easton picked out a few other things for me to try, and I tried not to skip with glee when I headed toward the fitting room.

"We'll be out here," Easton called as the employee hung the clothes on the little hook inside the fitting room and instructed me to let her know if I needed anything else.

As many fitting rooms were, it was hot, with the aggressive lights beating down on me, and the mirror was wholly unflattering. It was also a hell of a chore to remove the layers of clothes I'd put on, trying to stay warm in the brutal Colorado cold. But when I pushed the curtain aside and stepped out to show the boys—*my* boys—the blue dress, it was worth it.

Both of their eyes lit up, and I couldn't help my own smile. It fit really well and was as cozy as I expected.

I held my hands out to my sides and pushed up on my toes, spinning so they could take in the whole picture.

"What do we think?"

"It's perfect, P," Easton said.

"You're perfect," Liam added, and I'd never felt more beautiful than with both of their eyes on me.

Easton nudged Liam's arm, and he reluctantly looked away from me. "You trying to one-up me?"

Liam rolled his eyes. "Of course not. I just finally get to let the internal thoughts *out*. It's been ten years of keeping them all in."

Easton shot a wistful smile at me, one which I returned easily.

"We both get it. We all get to make up for lost time."

"Yes, we do. And on that note, let me try on the rest of this stuff, so we can go and *really* make up for all that lost time." With a wink, I sauntered back into the fitting room and tugged the curtain closed.

I pulled the dress off over my head and hung it back on the hanger when I heard one of the men groan.

"She's going to kill me," Liam said.

"Get used to it," Easton agreed. "You haven't seen the half of it yet."

thirteen

. . .

Palmer

IT REALLY WAS the perfect day, and I knew our night would be the icing on top of the immaculate cake.

Liam and Easton were laughing and joking around in our bedroom as I put the finishing touches on my makeup. I painted on my red lips and fluffed my hair, then straightened my leather jacket. I looked hot, which was nice, because that's what I was going for.

It was more modest than my skin-tight dress from last night, but I knew my men would love it.

My men, I thought again, rolling my eyes at my lovestruck reflection in the mirror.

Flipping the bathroom light off, I walked into the bedroom but stopped when I saw the looks on both their faces.

"What's wrong?" I asked quickly.

Liam's throat bobbed as he swallowed and tilted his phone my way. Nicole's name lit up the screen. That wasn't in the plan for our perfect day together.

"Answer it," Easton said, and Liam looked to me. All I could do was nod.

He glanced down and tapped the green button, but immediately put it on speakerphone.

"Hello?"

"Liam," Nicole sighed into the phone, and I hated how relieved her voice sounded.

Easton sat down in one of the chairs by the window and tugged me down with him. He positioned me on his lap and nuzzled his nose into my neck, kissing the tender place just below my ear. Goose bumps pebbled over my arms and down my legs, and I leaned into him.

"How are you?" Nicole asked, and Liam's hazel eyes flashed to us.

"I'm okay. How are you?"

She sighed again and went silent for several seconds before we heard her sniffle.

"Been better, but I was thinking about what you said when we talked yesterday. And I don't know…maybe when you're back in town, we should talk. Maybe I'd been too abrupt, breaking things off the way I did."

He dropped his head forward, and I watched his shoulders shrug with a deep breath. Easton's hand tightened on my waist, drawing little circles with his thumb over my skin just beneath my shirt.

He was trying to comfort me, but I could feel him tense beneath me.

"You think you want to get back together?" Liam asked, holding his phone out in one hand and shoving the other into the front pocket of his jeans.

"Maybe, yeah. Hell, I don't know. I just think we should talk in person when you're back, even if it's just for closure. I hate the way we left things."

"I don't know what to say." Liam sighed, and my heart was thumping a wild, uncontrollable beat. Maybe it was selfish, but I knew what he should say. He should tell her that he didn't want to reconsider, that he was moving on, and that was it.

"You don't have to answer me now. I only called to throw out the idea, but now that you've answered, I can hear in your voice that you might not be into the idea." There was a beat of silence, and when Liam didn't respond, Nicole added, "Am I right?"

"Yeah," Liam said. His voice was firm and held no argument. "You're right. I think...actually, I know that what you did was best for both of us. You just had the guts to do it when I didn't."

There was nothing but a faint shuffle on the other end of the phone, and we all waited in anticipatory silence.

"Well, I'm not going to beg for you back, or beg you to talk, so as long as you're sure?" she asked.

"Yeah, I'm sure."

"Okay, umm...bye, Liam."

"Bye, Nicole," Liam said and ended the call.

He tossed his phone onto the bed and spun on his heels, pacing away from us with his hands clasped behind his neck. Easton and I glanced at each other, and he gave me a nod, understanding exactly what I was silently asking.

I stood and crossed to Liam, running a hand up the center of his back.

"You okay?" I asked softly, and he dropped his hands. When he spun, there was a weary smile on his lips.

"Yeah," he said with a nod. "Just a little caught off-guard."

"Does getting her call...does it make you second-guess *us*?" I didn't want to sound selfish or make this about me, but I needed to know.

"No," Liam said automatically, cupping my cheeks and tilting my head back. "Never. I mean, I think there are some finer details we should probably discuss, but I'm not second-guessing that I seriously want to try this."

He leaned forward like he was going to kiss me but stopped just short. He glanced down at my lips and narrowed his eyes.

"If I kiss you, how badly am I going to fuck up this lipstick?"

"One kiss won't be the end of the world."

"I'll keep it chaste," he agreed and brushed his lips against mine. It was sweet and simple and not nearly what either of us needed, but he was sweet for trying to preserve my carefully applied makeup.

"Are we ready for drinks? Dinner?" Easton asked, stepping up beside us and wrapping an arm around Liam's shoulders.

"Yeah, let's go."

I couldn't stop giggling. Tequila wasn't usually my liquor of choice, but after tasting it on Liam's tongue last night, it was all I wanted. And I blamed my laughing fit on the tequila.

And the gorgeous men I was with.

I was seated between them at the bar, their hands intertwined on the back of my barstool. We'd received a few curious looks, a couple of people doing double-takes, trying to understand the dynamic, but no one was brave enough to stop by and ask.

An array of empty plates sat in front of us, and I could tell all three of us were eager to do something other than sit at the bar.

Easton's hand slid up my jean-clad thigh, and I shivered. Liam watched it happen under hungry, heavy-lidded eyes.

"Babe," I groaned, and Easton smiled deviously.

"She likes to be teased," he said over my head to Liam, who wore a very similar smile. "Although she pretends that she doesn't."

It was a love-hate relationship, really. I loved being teased because I knew what would come after. My husband never let me go without pleasure that rocked my world every time.

But now there were two of them, which meant double the teasing, and hopefully, double the pleasure. Because what was the point of having two men if that wasn't the outcome?

Kidding. Kinda.

Liam dropped his hand to my other thigh, and I flashed him a warning look that didn't contain any of the heat it could have.

All he did was smile and massage farther up my leg until I was squirming in my seat.

"Let's go upstairs," Easton whispered in my other ear, and Liam caught on and waved down the bartender. He requested the check, and while we waited, Easton drew torturous patterns over my thigh and under the bar where no one could see how close he was to an area that wasn't appropriate to touch in public.

Liam kept his hand firmly on my other thigh and dropped his mouth beside my ear. His warm breath swept over my skin, and I felt the heat everywhere.

"You're so fucking perfect, Sparky. You've been my dream girl since I first saw you at that party." I stuttered a short breath into my aching lungs. "The things I want to do to you…I can't wait to watch you writhing on my cock, feel you pulsing around me and screaming out my name. You think you can do that for me?"

"Scream your name when I come?" I asked in a breathy voice.

Liam nodded, and so did I, my eyes skimming over his beautiful, rugged features and settling on his full lips.

"Make me scream, and I'll make sure it's your name falling from my lips."

His smile was all devious promise, and we were locked in a heated stare down when Easton cleared his throat from my other side.

"Bill's paid. Let's go before you two start fucking on the top of the bar."

Liam and I were both out of our chairs in an instant, following Easton through the lobby and to the elevator bank. I was so grateful that our room was only a short elevator ride away.

We stepped in with another older couple, and it was miserable trying to keep our hands to ourselves.

But once Easton slipped the key over the pad and pushed open the door, all bets were off.

fourteen

. . .

Palmer

I WAS first through the door and walked backward so I could watch the two gorgeous men prowl toward me.

Desire surged through me, and I couldn't help but smile. My legs hit the bed, and I sat clumsily down as Liam kept moving. In my peripheral, Easton shrugged off his jacket, but Liam stepped between my legs and towered over me. His fingers twisted in the back of my hair while his other hand cupped my cheek, guiding me into a deep, soul-crushing kiss that I felt all the way down to my toes.

And that was all he did before he stepped back next to Easton. They both looked down at me, and my chest heaved with each breath I managed to suck in.

Fuck, I was so wet and more turned on than I could ever remember.

Liam slowly lifted his eyes to Easton, heat filling his hazel stare.

"You have to show me what she likes, Easton. Show me how to please your wife."

"Fuck, yes. By the time we're done, you'll be an expert in her pleasure too."

Both of their gazes landed on me again, and Easton moved. He pushed my legs wide and stepped between them, his touch unforgiving and purposeful. He shoved my leather jacket off my arms and tugged my top over my head. He threw them both to the floor on the other side of the bed and dropped to his knees.

I could feel Liam watching our entire interaction, but I was solely focused on my husband, who unzipped one boot, then the other. Boots gone and left in nothing but my black, lace bra—one I only wore on special occasions because, honestly, it was incredibly uncomfortable—Easton reached for my belt, and with expert hands slid it open and unzipped my jeans.

He stripped the denim down my legs, and I realized, for the first time, I was almost completely naked in front of both of them. Of course, my panties matched my bra, because I hoped something like this would happen. I was prepared.

All my clothes gone, Easton stood once again next to Liam, and they both took their eye full. I'd never felt more desired or beautiful with their heated, longing-filled eyes raking over me.

My skin felt like every nerve ending was exposed, and I was panting when Liam reached below his belt and ran a harsh hand over his growing erection.

Easton laced his fingers through Liam's and stepped forward, urging him to fit between my legs. My hands flat on the bed behind me, I tilted my head back.

Easton reached forward and brushed that secret place just below my ear that made me see stars.

"Kiss her here," he instructed, and Liam did as he asked. I moaned as he kissed me.

"Good, now lower," Easton said, and Liam didn't hesitate to move or listen to exactly the instructions Easton provided. He motioned to my collarbone, to the space between my breasts, down my stomach, and on the inside of each thigh.

While Liam burned a teasing path down my body, lips

lingering and sucking sweetly on my skin, Easton stood behind him. He touched Liam anywhere and everywhere. Hands skimming over his wide shoulders and up his toned stomach, they finally cupped Liam's thick cock, bulging from behind his jeans, and the pleasure coiling inside me felt like it was about to explode.

Liam moaned against my skin, lips brushing against the inside of my knee, and canting his hips harder into Easton's touch.

It was so fucking hot, Easton telling Liam what to do and how to touch me, all while touching him.

"You're going to make me come," Liam growled against my skin, and Easton just laughed.

"A little quick on the trigger?" he joked, and Liam moaned.

He stood to his full height and turned to Easton, clasping his cheeks and pressing a searing kiss to his mouth.

Easton gave as good as he got. They both fought for dominance, ripping at each other's clothing and trying to direct the kiss at the same time. It was all teeth, tongues, and growls, and I was living for it.

Dropping back to one elbow, I propped my feet on the edge of the bed and spread my legs. I licked my middle and ring fingers and pushed past my panties. The first swipe of fingers against my clit made my hips surge forward. Even though it was my hand, I still felt the intense pleasure start rising to its peak.

"Look at her," Liam grunted with his hand around Easton's throat. "She's watching us with her pretty little fingers against her pussy."

Easton groaned, and I dipped my fingers lower.

"Fuck, sweet girl," Easton panted, running his hand down Liam's stomach and shoving past the waistband of his black briefs. Liam's eyes rolled back, and my breath hitched when Easton dropped to his knees.

He tugged Liam's briefs down, and his hard, thick cock sprang free. A generous bead of precum collected at his flared head. Easton licked his lips, and I didn't want to blink for fear I'd miss anything.

He leaned forward and flattened his tongue on Liam's head, collecting the precum. He closed his eyes like he was savoring the taste before he quickly dove back in. Easton's lips fitted around Liam's shaft, and he sucked. *Hard.*

Liam's head dropped back as he fisted Easton's short hair. But like he too couldn't keep his eyes averted, Liam looked back down at my husband on his knees at his feet.

I rubbed my clit harder and whimpered at the pleasure. Liam's hooded eyes shot to me, and a smile slipped across his lips.

"Look at how turned on your wife is, East. How much she likes watching her husband suck his best friend's cock."

Easton popped off Liam's cock for a moment, still shuttling his hand up and down his thick length, and only long enough to say, "Come here."

His deep voice was filled with delicious command. I slid off the bed, dropping to my knees next to Easton and looking up at Liam. His jaw went slack, and his other hand cupped my cheek.

Easton pushed himself all the way down Liam until his nose was buried in his tidy dark blond hair at the base of his cock. Liam shoved himself deeper, making Easton gag and spit drip down his chin.

"Fuck, yes," I muttered. I gripped Easton's thigh and dug my nails into his skin. And fuck, it was so hot, but I wasn't as much of a voyeur as East. I wanted to be a part of every single moment. Or at least most of them.

So I leaned forward and dragged my tongue against Easton's lower lip and Liam's soft skin. They both groaned, and I moved lower. I sucked one of his heavy balls into my mouth and reveled in the soap and salt taste of him.

Liam cursed, and Easton leaned back. With lips that were wet from sucking his best friend's cock, he kissed me soundly. His free hand, that wasn't wrapped around Liam, cupped the other side of my face and urged my lips apart. I tasted the remnants of Liam on his tongue, and I wanted more.

Like he knew exactly what I was thinking, he let me go with one final kiss and guided me toward Liam's waiting cock. I replaced my hand around his wet shaft and stared up his strong body as I leaned forward and slipped his cock into my mouth.

My tongue circled his thick head, and I massaged my hand up and down his length.

"Yes, just like that," Liam forced out through gritted teeth.

"That's my good girl," Easton murmured, running his hand down my back as I pushed Liam deeper. "Gag on his cock. I know you can go deeper than that."

Never one to back down from a challenge, and knowing he was right, I forced him deeper until I felt his tip nudge the back of my throat, and I couldn't help but gag around him.

But I pushed through and held him deep. My eyes watered, and Liam's image blurred above me as Easton whispered how good I was and how proud of me he was.

"Fuck her mouth," Easton instructed. He wound his fingers in the back of my hair, holding my head steady for Liam, who smiled down at me.

"My pleasure," he growled, thrusting forward and forcing me to swallow around him. Liam held the top of my head and fucked my mouth with reckless abandon.

The sounds coming from my mouth were obscene, and I was growing wetter with every thrust. I loved how it felt to be used for their pleasure, and I wanted more.

I *needed* more.

With the two men holding me in place, my hand was free to drop between my legs. I pushed my panties to the side and dragged my fingers against my clit. But the second my pleasure spiked, my fingers were batted out of the way and replaced with much larger ones.

I whimpered and moaned around Liam's cock, and I was seconds away and a few expert strokes against my clit before I was shattering. My hearing muffled, and the edges of my vision went dark with the incredible intensity of the orgasm.

And I couldn't take anymore. With one tap against Liam's thigh, he let me go, and I sucked in a much-needed breath.

"Fuck me," I panted. "Use me, please. Both of you."

fifteen

. . .

Liam

NEVER HAD MORE glorious words been uttered. The second the plea was out of Palmer's wet lips, Easton was moving. He reached for her, and they both stood, but not for long. He cradled her under her ass and lifted her into his arms. The tight muscles in his biceps and forearms flexed as he walked the few feet to the bed and dropped her right on the edge.

She bounced with a gasp.

"Don't move," he growled and paced to the other side of the room.

All I could do was stand there and watch them. It was easy, the way they moved together, but I didn't feel left out. Honestly, it felt like a gift to be able to watch two people so in love that being together was as easy as breathing for them.

Easton was busy sifting through one of their suitcases in the corner, and I could tell by the smile on Palmer's face that she must have known what was coming.

Her perfectly applied eye makeup was running in black streaks down her face, and I wondered if we could make her cry again. I might be a sadistic fuck, but it was a beautiful sight, both of them crying and gagging on my cock at my feet.

My cock kicked at the reminder, and I gritted my teeth together. Lasting much longer was going to be a feat.

Easton turned back to us, long, hard dick bobbing with each step, that I almost missed what he had in his hand. He pointed the blue wand vibrator at Palmer with an evil smile.

"How about this, sweet girl?" he began, stopping beside me. "We use this and take turns fucking your pretty little cunt. Every time you come, we switch."

"For how long?" she asked in a voice that was so breathy that it was barely there. She was leaning back on her elbows, feet propped on the edge of the bed, and legs bent. She'd disposed of her panties, and I was awarded a perfect view of her. Her pussy was dripping and swollen, ready to be fucked just after her orgasm.

"How long do you think, Liam?" Easton turned to me, and my smile matched the devious intent burning in his eyes.

I gazed back down at Palmer, who was breathing hard, cheeks red, and eyes bouncing between the two of us.

"If she wants to be used, then we use her for as long as we want."

"Perfect answer," Easton agreed and turned, bracing a hand around the back of my neck and kissing me handily. It didn't last long, but it was powerful nonetheless. My entire body thrummed with excitement.

He stepped back and motioned to Palmer.

"Would you like to go first?"

Licking my lips, Palmer shrugged off her bra and tossed it to the side of the bed with the rest of her clothes. Her perfect, rounded tits with dusky pink nipples were begging to be sucked and nipped.

"No, you go ahead. Show me how your wife likes to be fucked."

Easton groaned and let his hungry gaze roam over me before

he stepped between Palmer's legs. He bent down and kissed her softly. It was nothing like I expected with the plan he'd formed for us.

Rounding him, I gripped my cock in my fist as he clicked a few buttons, and the vibrator came to life in his hand.

"You know we love you, right?" he asked, and Palmer nodded emphatically. "Good, because we're about to fuck you like we don't."

We. We love you.

There was no other warning. He dropped the rounded head of the toy to her clit and slammed home. Her scream was filled with pleasure and tinged with pain.

Easton's cock disappeared inside her snug cunt, and he yelled out a deep curse.

They both were still for a moment, bodies adjusting to the barrage of sensations, but it wasn't more than that—a moment—and then Easton began moving.

His first thrusts were slow and deep. He ground into her, and I realized my hand on my cock was moving at the same speed, like it was me fucking her too.

Her hands dropped back behind her head, and she scrambled for the sheets, for something to hold on to while her husband pounded into her.

It wasn't long enough. I barely got to watch the way the muscles in Easton's back flexed and the way Palmer's back arched before she was screaming out another all-consuming release.

Easton's thrusts stopped, and his expression turned pained as he held off his own orgasm.

He didn't give her a second's rest. He took a staggering step back and handed me the toy. I glanced from it to her and took my place between her shaking legs.

I lined up with her cunt but stopped. "Condom?" I asked no one in particular.

"Up to you, sweet girl," Easton said, standing beside me and running a hand over her leg. "I got them just in case, but—"

"No," she said quickly. She sat up, her weight on her hands behind her, and her breath coming out in quick, short pants. "I want to feel you, Liam. I've been waiting too long not to feel you bare. And I have an IUD, so unless you think we should, then—"

Her words cut off in a gasp as I pushed inside her. I think my answer was clear enough, although every one of my thoughts weren't so clear after her inner walls clamped around me.

The enormity of the moment was sitting heavily in my chest, and I couldn't will myself to move. I was having a threesome with my best friends—with my *married* best friends—and they wanted me to be part of their relationship.

That's what they wanted, right? Because I was balls deep in Palmer, and I don't think I could ever go back to before. They were mine, and I was theirs.

But still, I couldn't move. Paralyzed by how much I wanted them, Easton sidled up next to me. He wrapped his hand around mine that was still holding the vibrator and lowered it to Palmer's clit. She jumped and pulsed around me.

"Oh, *fuck*," I cried and peered down at where I impaled her, slack-jawed and fucking amazed.

Easton dropped his mouth to my ear and kissed my neck. "Use my wife," he said, but then added, "Fuck our girl just how she wants us to."

And he pressed a searing kiss to my lips as I began to fuck our girl.

"Yes, yes, yes," Palmer chanted, and I could feel the vibration through my shaft. We both looked down at her, and Easton took hold of the vibrator as I gripped both of Palmer's hips. "Harder."

She didn't have to ask me twice. I slammed into her harder, but just as deep.

"Is he fucking you just right, sweet girl?" Easton asked, and Palmer nodded. Her eyes screwed shut, her pussy clamped down around me, and I could feel the beginning of her orgasm. She squeezed me so tight, I didn't know if I'd be able to hold off. But I clenched my jaw and rode out her screaming orgasm with every bit of restraint I had left.

And if I hadn't pulled out of her when I did, I wouldn't have made it another round.

sixteen

. . .

Easton

WATCHING another man fuck your wife might not be for everyone. I never thought it would be for me. And I knew it wouldn't be if it were any other man.

But it was Liam who was making Palmer come for the sixth time. It was my best friend who held her down as her legs shook, and she reached for the vibrator, trying to tear it away.

"Fuck, sweet girl, you're going to make me come," he groaned. Tears streaked down Palmer's pink cheeks, and Liam looked at her with all the care in the world as he fucked her mercilessly.

I was standing beside them, stroking my cock in time with his thrusts, and at the point of coming myself, just watching the two of them together.

Liam's blond hair, damp with sweat, had fallen down in front of his face, but I came up behind him and fisted enough of it in my hand to wrench his head back. I notched my cock in the warm seam of his ass and held onto his hip with my free hand.

"Do it," I growled in his ear. "Come inside our girl. Pump her so full she'll feel you dripping out of her for a week."

"Yes, please," Palmer begged. "Fill me up, Liam. Please, *please*."

His body tensed, and then he roared, stilling inside her and pumping her full. Palmer gasped, and I caught her eye over his shoulder. No words were needed. I knew she was having the time of her life. I knew she was thinking the same thing I was—we were never going back. He was ours.

Liam's hips began moving again, and my cock nudged his ass with every thrust. Exhausted, he dropped his head back onto my shoulder and tilted his face to mine.

"Your turn," he offered, his voice gravelly with lust.

I kissed him, and he slipped free. But I quickly took his place inside Palmer, not wanting any little bit of his cum to drip free.

The combination of the two of them—Palmer's multiple orgasms and Liam's thick cum—was too perfect. I turned the vibrator up one more time, and Palmer's tears began anew.

"East, I can't. I can't…" she pleaded, but I shook my head.

"Yes, you can. You can do it for me. For us. You know what to say to make it stop."

"Lasagna" had been our safe word for as long as we'd been together. It was what I'd been cooking for her the first time we'd had sex, so it just stuck.

She'd said it a few times before, but she didn't utter it now. Her tears were in freefall, and I looked to my right to see Liam staring down at her with utter adoration.

He swept a big hand through his disheveled hair and caught me looking. One step, and his chest was pressed against my arm.

"Both of you," he snarled through clenched teeth. "Come for me."

He gripped my throat, and it was such a foreign sensation, having someone with hands big enough to effectively wrap around my neck and impede my airway.

And I was a prisoner to his command. Palmer tightened around me and screamed into the quiet room. My own release wasn't far behind. Liam's eyes locked on mine. He didn't miss a moment of the pleasure that washed over my face.

I felt like I'd been shot into space, my body floating in never-ending satisfaction until his kiss grounded me again. Turning off the toy, I tossed it on the side of the bed, and Liam and I both went to work making sure Palmer was okay.

He lifted her into his arms, and I followed them into the spacious shower. We washed each other, kissing and touching without the intent of taking it further. It was intimate with the lights low and the warm water rushing over us.

Of course, neither Liam nor I was neglected, but we made Palmer our focus. We showered her with praise, making sure she knew how perfect she was for us and how much we enjoyed it.

By the time we crawled into bed, all of us clean and satisfied, sleep was imminent.

Palmer was the first to succumb. She was squeezed between Liam and me, her head resting on his chest, and I was curved around her back. Our hands were intertwined, and she looked instantly peaceful with a smile on her face.

"That was…" Liam began, but trailed off.

"Amazing," I finished for him, and he smiled.

"Who knew you were such a good cocksucker," he quipped, and I nipped at his shoulder. We both laughed quietly and fell into a tired, companionable silence.

My eyes drifted shut, and I dozed off for a while, only to open my eyes and find Liam staring at the ceiling.

Reaching over, I brushed a lock of blond hair out of his face and drew his attention away from the blank ceiling.

"You're thinking too loud," I whispered.

He forced a small smile. "I'll try to keep it down."

"Tell me, baby."

The pet name slipped free, and Liam's eyes softened.

"I want this to be real," he said slowly. Without any more explanation, I knew exactly what he meant, because I'd had the same thought. It felt too good to be true.

"It is real."

But he shook his head. Carefully, though, so as not to disturb the sleeping Palmer on his chest. We both glanced down at her, and I hoped she felt lucky to have two men who were crazy about her.

He sighed and brushed his lips against the top of her head. "It feels real right now, but what about when we get back to the *real* world? Everything is perfect when we're in our own little bubble at this beautiful resort, but I mean, have you thought about what your parents are going to say? Or how this will work when you go back home and I'm back in my apartment? Or—"

"Liam," I whispered quickly. He stopped talking, and I hated the doubt clouding his features, or what I could see of his features in the dim bedroom light. "My parents already love you, and I know they would be accepting. Same for Palmer's parents. Hell, they were in a throuple for years."

"And the rest of it?" he asked, just a touch too loudly. Palmer stirred between us, and we both froze as she curled back into Liam's side.

"I'm really not worried about it. We will figure it out."

"How do you know that?"

"Because we want to. We want to figure it out, so we will. Right?"

Tender hazel eyes met mine, and he let his head fall back onto his pillow. "I really want to."

Lifting my free hand, the one that wasn't tucked around Palmer, I dragged my fingers through his hair. He softened under my touch, and his eyelids fluttered closed.

"I do too," I muttered as he fell asleep. "I do too."

seventeen

. . .

Palmer

I WAS safe and cozy when I woke up, but I was also extremely hot. Kicking the comforter off, the cool air felt amazing against my warm skin.

My eyes fluttered open, and I noticed Easton still peacefully asleep next to me, cuddled in a mound of white sheets and bedding. But the other side of the bed was empty. Rolling out of bed, I peered at the clock across the room. It wasn't even seven yet, but I heard the shower running down the hall.

I rubbed the sleep from my eyes and quietly padded down the hallway.

The bathroom door was slightly ajar, faint light spilling out from the crack at the bottom and sides. The humid air lingered with the deep, woodsy smell of the body wash Liam and Easton had been using the past few days.

I pushed the door open and slipped inside, shutting it silently behind me.

The tile floor was warm on my bare feet, and I stood against the counter across from the glass shower. It was fogged, but I could still see Liam. Standing under the rainfall showerhead, his head was tilted back, his hand in his blond hair, and his muscles flexed. The water ran down his body, and my eyes followed its glorious path.

His cock was still impressive, even soft, and arousal pooled in my lower stomach with the reminder of how good he felt inside me.

I was too caught up in the memories that I didn't realize Liam had spotted me until he gasped.

"Fuck, Sparky. You scared the shit out of me," he said with a startled laugh. He reached forward and scrubbed some of the condensation from the glass, giving me a better view of his gorgeous, hard face. "Did I wake you? I tried to be as quiet as possible. I thought about using my shower, but all my stuff is in here."

"Because this is your shower too," I said, smiling. "And no, you didn't wake me. Easton is a freaking furnace. That's what woke me up."

"I'm almost done, but you can hop in with me if you want," Liam offered, and I knew that a shower with him would be hot and that we likely would get very dirty before we got clean. But I was enjoying the view.

He scrubbed a hand through his generous stubble and pushed his hair out of his face.

"I don't know," I mused. I didn't try to hide the way my eyes dropped down his body or how much I appreciated it. "I'm really kind of enjoying my view right here."

Making my decision, I pressed up onto the counter behind me. It was a few degrees cooler than the surrounding air and chilled the exposed skin on my legs. My panties didn't do much in the way of protection.

"You gonna watch me finish showering?"

I nodded and crossed my legs in front of me. "I haven't ogled openly for almost a decade, so I have to make up for lost time. Unless it bothers you?"

Liam shook his head and squirted some conditioner into his hand.

"Bother me? No, absolutely not. It'll turn me on, though."

Folding my hands in my lap, my smile widened, and that arousal from before was growing harder to ignore.

"What a shame," I quipped. "So why are you up so early?"

He scrubbed the conditioner into his hair and shrugged. "I… umm…I'm just an early riser." If he hadn't averted his eyes immediately, I might have questioned whether I'd heard the waver in his voice. But together, I knew he was lying.

I flattened my palms on either side of my crossed legs and watched him rinse his hands under the water.

"I know you are," I said. "But I also know that's not the truth."

He cut his eyes in my direction, and his massive shoulders dropped. Whatever it was, it was eating him up, but I tried to remain patient. Liam had always needed to come to things in his own time and on his own terms. He internalized much more than Easton or me. We were external processors and immediately talked about everything.

"You fell asleep pretty quick last night," he said just above the sound of the water. "But East and I were up for a while longer, talking…"

"Talking…" I prompted, hoping he would continue.

"This sounds so fucking stupid, but honestly, Sparky, I'm scared."

My heart broke at the pain in his voice, and my entire being begged me to jump into his arms and placate any doubts or concerns.

"Why?" was all I could manage to ask, and my voice cracked over the word.

He stepped back under the water and washed the conditioner out of his hair. It only took a few seconds, but it felt like forever. He squeezed the excess water out of his hair and rubbed a hand over his face before shutting the water off and grabbing the towel over the door.

He didn't speak again until he was standing on the rug and tying the towel around his waist.

"Because I want this so bad," he finally said. "I want this so bad, it hurts, and I'm worried it's not going to work."

I was about to slip off the counter and reach for him, but he took two steps and stopped in front of me. I had to touch him. It felt wrong not to, and I flattened both my hands against his tense stomach muscles. They flexed under my fingers, and his eyes dropped to my hands.

"This is going to work," I said, hoping my confidence translated. Because I was confident. "I know it will, because I've only ever felt this way once before, and it was when I met the man still sleeping in the other room. We want you, Liam. We want *this*."

"That's what East said too."

I smiled. Of course he did. We'd discussed it and knew exactly what we wanted. We wouldn't have pursued it without agreement, but there also wasn't a world in which we wouldn't have.

"I don't doubt that," I said. "But I'm not going to blow smoke up your ass. It might be *work*. A polyamorous relationship isn't the easiest for the world to accept, and there might be some awkward or uncomfortable moments while we try to navigate it."

My parents had been in a relationship with another woman for a while, and they'd experienced their share of hate and nonacceptance. It had been before I was born, but they'd kept photographs from that time and talked openly about their experiences.

They hadn't hidden how ugly the world could be, or how the relationship had helped them grow.

"But it's nothing we can't handle."

Liam leaned forward and brushed his lips against mine, settling his hands on my hips and humming deep in his throat.

"I like how confident you sound," he muttered, dropping his forehead to mine.

I kissed him again, but it wasn't pretty because I couldn't stop smiling. I placed my hands on either side of his face and loved the scrape of his stubble against my palms.

"I am confident," I agreed. "And I'll be as confident as I need to be for the three of us. We'll figure it all out. I already know I want you to move in when we get home. I can't go from seeing you every second of every day to living apart again."

Liam scoffed out a broken laugh and shook his head. He leaned back just enough that he could look down at me. "Is that so? You talked to East about this?"

I shrugged. The concern in his hazel eyes had been replaced with excitement, and I reveled in it. "Easton will agree with whatever I say, especially if it means you with us more often or all the time. Also, he knows that there is some truth to the saying, 'Happy spouse, happy house.'"

"I'd do anything if it makes you happy, Sparky." Then he kissed me again, which was good, because otherwise he would have seen the tears beginning to gather in my eyes.

Our kiss wasn't chaste or sweet for long. His grip tightened on my hips, and I twisted my fingers in his damp hair. He plunged his tongue against my mouth, and I uncrossed my legs, scooting to the edge of the counter and pressing us closer together.

He moaned when the apex of my thighs brushed his dick, which was impressively tenting the white towel around his waist. My hand blazed a path down his neck, his chest, and stomach, intent on gripping his cock, but he beat me to it. He covered my hands with his, stopping them, and pulled back.

"You know what's so wrong?" he asked, and I shook my head. "I know how you feel coming around my fingers and my cock, but I haven't had the pleasure of tasting you yet."

"Yes," I keened.

"You want that too?"

"Yes," I repeated more urgently the second time.

"Then spread your legs, sweet girl. Show me your perfect cunt."

His dirty words made me shiver, and I didn't hesitate to do exactly as he requested. I scooted back just enough that I could plant my feet on the counter and lean back with my weight on my hands behind me.

Liam's deep, hazel eyes hungrily swept over me, and he palmed his cock over the towel. His stare was like a caress I could feel across my skin. It was enough to make me dizzy. Quickly, he grabbed the hem of my shirt—*his* shirt, actually—and tugged it over my head.

He dropped his mouth to the center of my chest and placed a hot, open-mouth kiss between my breasts. My body shook, and I stuttered a gasp when his lips closed around one of my nipples. Twisting my fingers in his hair, pleasure coiled through me.

He sucked hard, twirling his tongue skillfully around the peak, and giving me the briefest hint of what was to come between my legs. With the barest graze of his teeth, my hips surged forward, searching for release and relief.

He switched to my other breast and replaced his mouth with his fingers on the other. He sucked and kneaded and drove me so crazy, mumbled pleas fell from my lips.

"Please?" he asked, pulling back and licking his lips. "Tell me what you want, sweet girl."

"Put your mouth on me. Lick my pussy, and please make me come."

"I would be honored," he purred, kissing a hot trail down the center of my body. Unbothered by my wet panties, he continued over the top of the fabric and down my slit. His big hands flattened on the inside of my thighs and pushed them down toward the counter. The stretch felt good, and I was obscenely open for him.

"There's already a wet spot right here," he said and blew against my damp panties. I panted and fought against his hold to move my hips, but it was useless. He was so much stronger than me, holding me down with a small part of his full strength. He kissed the wet spot, then stripped my panties down my legs.

I didn't care where they went. All I cared about was that his hands landed on my thighs again and pressed them to the counter.

"Fuck, I love your pussy. Your clit is already swollen, like it's begging to be sucked and licked. And the rest of your cunt is pretty and puffy. God, it's perfect, and I bet it's going to taste just as good."

The first brush of his tongue was one long lick from my ass to my clit, and I cried out into the silent bathroom.

"Shh, sweet girl," Liam muttered as he licked me again. "You're going to wake up your husband, and he's going to walk in here to find his best friend eating his wife's cunt."

He dropped to his knees and speared his tongue inside me with a low chuckle. "Then again, maybe that's what you want. The way you just gushed around my tongue makes me think you'd like that."

My body reacted before my lust-addled thoughts could catch up. But yes, I loved the way that sounded. I liked how dirty it was and how wrong it was supposed to be. I liked when Liam called me Easton's wife, similar to how I loved when Easton said it himself.

Flattening his tongue, he ground it against my clit and eased one thick finger inside me at the same time. His free hand gripped under my ass and kneaded my flesh as my hips started moving of their own accord. And however I moved, he took it easily.

He held me firmly to his mouth and didn't let up until I was nearly screaming out my release. I dug my nails into the counter beneath me as my back bowed, and that coiling pleasure exploded.

My head hit the mirror behind me, but I couldn't care about the twinge of pain. I heaved out a breath as aftershocks rocked my body.

"Fuck, Liam," I muttered, and he leaned back with a smile. My orgasm coated his mouth, and he kissed me one last time.

"You taste better than I thought," he said.

"You and East both say that, but I know you're lying."

"No, we're not." My head jerked to my left, where Easton was leaning against the doorframe. Neither Liam nor I had heard the door open, but I wasn't surprised we hadn't—we were a little busy.

Easton's arms were crossed over his bare chest, his plaid pajama pants hanging low on his hips. My legs still spread, Easton pushed off the doorframe and strode toward us. He stopped in front of Liam and glanced down at my exposed pussy, a dark desire forming behind his eyes. His jaw tensed as he licked his lips and looked back at Liam. His white towel was still tented, but Easton paid it no mind.

Easton's hand struck out and closed around Liam's throat and tugged him into a deep kiss that would weaken anyone's knees. No doubt East tasted me on Liam's lips, and they both groaned in satisfaction. Just as Liam was reaching for him, Easton pulled back and licked his lips again.

"We're snowboarding, remember? Gotta leave in twenty." And he strode out of the room.

eighteen

. . .

Liam

EASTON WAS SO good at everything. Literally *everything*.

I was all right at snowboarding, and Palmer was getting the hang of it after years of spending time on the mountain with Easton's family. But East was fucking killer.

Which was why we'd enlisted him to go pick up food while Palmer returned some work emails, and I took advantage of the hot tub on our back deck. I dropped my towel on one of the patio chairs and immediately hopped into the water. It was too fucking cold to be outside in anything less than a thick coat, but the warm, rolling water was the perfect temperature, especially to soothe my tired, sore muscles.

I sank lower into the water and tried to clear my mind, only for my phone to begin buzzing where I had left it on the edge of the hot tub. Groaning, I glanced at it quickly and decided to ignore it if it wasn't important.

My heart collided with my rib cage when I realized it was Easton's mom's name scrolling across the screen.

I tried to dry off my hand and quickly jammed the green button. "Hello?"

"Hi, Liam, it's Margaret Winters."

I chuckled softly. "I know. I have your number saved, Mrs. Winters."

I heard her scoff, and I knew what was coming. "We've known each other long enough now, Liam. Please call me Margaret, or Margie."

"I'm sorry, but I'm not sure I can do that," I said honestly. "My mom would have had my butt if I didn't call you Mrs. Winters."

"Fair enough," she said, and I could hear the soft smile in her voice. "So how is your vacation going? As relaxing as you'd hoped it would be?"

"For the most part. The beginning was a little rough, but it's going well…now."

She was quiet for a beat, and I looked down at my phone to make sure the call hadn't dropped.

I put it back to my ear just as she said, "Easton told me about your breakup. I'm so sorry, Liam. We thought Nicole was a lovely girl."

"She is, she is," I mumbled, running my free hand over the top of the bubbling water. "And I appreciate it, but I'm doing well. It was for the best. No doubt."

"Well, yes, now that you're finally with Easton and Palmer, right?"

I sat bolt upright and almost dropped my phone into the water. If I thought my pulse was racing before, I thought I might be having a heart attack the longer I considered her words.

"Wha-what?" I stuttered.

She laughed, and although the sound was light and sweet, it didn't do much to assuage my concern.

"I know you must be…what does Palmer call it…*shitting yourself,* so I'll just say that David and I are overjoyed. You know we love you, and we couldn't be happier, as long as you three are happy."

Words were impossible to find. I stammered and mumbled and was lost in a chaos of thoughts.

"I just wanted you to know that, and we can't wait to celebrate when you get back home."

"Umm…thank you. I really appreciate that."

She said a quick goodbye and hung up the phone. Slowly, I set it back down on the edge of the hot tub and tried to wrap my mind around the short conversation.

They knew, which means someone told them, and I had a very good idea who it was.

And like my thoughts had willed him to appear, Easton, wearing an adorable black beanie, a giant puffy coat, and a wide grin, pushed through the sliding glass door. The air around his breath fogged, and he swung his green eyes to me.

"Food's here," he said, motioning with his thumb back toward the room. But his face dropped quickly, and he stepped farther onto the deck. "What's wrong?"

I guess my expression didn't hide my confusion and wide range of emotions as well as I thought it might.

"You told them," I said a little more caustically than I intended. "You told your parents."

He pushed the door closed behind him and paced toward me. "Sorry, she's on the phone. But yeah, I told them. Well, I called my mom, and we talked."

"What did you tell her exactly?" I asked and stood, not even caring that the air was much cooler and hurt my skin.

"I told her that this is real. That the three of us—me, you, and Palmer—are in a relationship. That you're just as important to me as she is, and vice versa. And she reacted exactly like I expected, Liam. She is happy as long as we are. I didn't expect her to immediately call you, though."

"Well, she did," I quipped. I planted one hand on my hip and ran the other through my hair.

Easton strode farther across the deck, stopping just at the edge of the hot tub and directly in front of me.

"Why do you sound angry? I didn't mean—"

"I know, and I don't know." I sighed. All the emotions rolling through me presented as anger for some reason. It was a lot to decipher, and I wasn't the best at dealing with such an onslaught of feelings. But with Easton standing in front of me, looking like a hurt puppy dog, I felt like I had to get there quicker. I had to figure my shit out.

The cold had finally seeped down to my bones, and I shivered. Easton glanced around and found my towel on the patio chair. He unraveled it and tossed it over my shoulders.

"Do you wanna go inside?"

"No," I said. "No, no. I…just give me a second." I braced my hands on the edge of the tub and dropped my head forward. He'd taken my concerns to heart and done his best to allay them. His intentions were pure, and I never doubted that at least.

But I hadn't been completely honest about everything I was feeling.

"You, your family, Palmer—you're the only family I have left," I said quietly. "If this doesn't work, East, I'm not going to be okay if I lose you all." I stared down at the bubbling water as I spoke. "I can't lose you guys."

A heavy silence followed, but not for long. Easton's boots appeared in my periphery, and his hands cupped my face. He urged me to look up, but I also wasn't going to fight him.

I straightened and was met with sincere green eyes. His palms were warm against my cool skin, and I couldn't *not* give in to his touch.

His gaze bounced between mine, and the longer we stood there, the more my nerves eased. He licked his lips and took a deep breath.

"You're never going to lose us. We could never let you go."

"Even if—"

"Even if we don't work out romantically—which I would bet all the money in the world that we will—you will not lose us. You can't."

And fuck, I believed him.

"Okay," I said quietly, and the fear in his expression transformed with the easy smile that graced his lips.

"So you're all in?"

My hands dropped to his hips, and I weaved my way under his coat. He stepped closer and didn't appear to care about getting wet as the water bubbled between us.

"Yeah, I'm all in," I agreed, and he slammed his mouth to mine. Tightening his grip on me, I deepened the kiss, tracing his lips with my tongue and savoring the groan that let me in.

Everything else completely forgotten, I shoved his coat off his shoulders and began working his belt open as he tossed his shirt to the ground and stepped out of his boots.

In only black briefs, he easily climbed into the hot tub without breaking our kiss. He wrapped an arm around my waist and backed us into the corner I'd claimed before.

We dipped back down into the warm water, and I sat on the seat as Easton stepped between my legs. He leaned his forehead against mine, and we both tried to catch our breath. He laughed low in his throat, and I couldn't contain my smile. His nose brushed mine, and I stole another quick kiss.

"I love you, Liam," Easton said, and my breath caught in my throat. I'd heard those words before, but they were usually followed by "man" or "bro" and were meant in a like-a-brother-type of way. That wasn't the way he said it now, though.

His voice was low and ragged, and his fingers massaged the bare skin at my waist.

"Let me rephrase," he continued. "I'm *in* love with you, Liam Taylor. It's kind of pathetic how much I love you."

"Not pathetic," I growled and tugged him closer. It was hard to kiss him when I couldn't stop fucking smiling, but I was a million pounds lighter just hearing him say it. Hearing him voice the exact feelings I'd felt for years was better than I ever expected. "And if you're pathetic, so am I, because fuck, East, I'm in love with you too. I have been since the day I met you."

He leaned back and smiled down at me. "Hell yeah, you are."

"So fucking cocky," I muttered between more kisses.

"Sure, but you love it."

I laughed and launched myself off the little seat, pinning him in the opposite corner. He let out a startled gasp with the impact but smiled, like I knew he would.

"But," he began, nipping at my lips and pressing his fingers to my waistband before dropping lower and squeezing my cock through my swimsuit. "Maybe you could fuck it out of me tonight?"

"You want me to…"

"Fuck the cocky out of me, yes," he said simply.

His words by themselves would have me hard up, but with his palm around my dick? I felt like I was going to explode. My jaw clenched, and I rolled my hips up into his touch.

"I might have to fuck you more than once. At least a couple of times to really make an impact."

His laugh was throaty and deep.

"Well, good thing we have forever then."

nineteen

. . .

Easton

We were going to play out one of my all-time fantasies, a fantasy I'd had since my junior year of high school.

Liam was going to fuck me, and I was going to enjoy every second of it.

"Have you done this before?" he asked, and I shook my head.

"No. If I was going to bottom, I wanted you to be the first."

He groaned and tilted his head back to the dark sky above us. Little snowflakes had begun to fall while I was confessing my feelings to the boy I'd loved for fifteen years.

He looked back down at me, and little flakes clung to his dark lashes. His pupils were blown wide as he cupped my cheek and ran his thumb across my lower lip.

"I'm honored," he muttered. "Now, you think you can handle the cold so I can suck your cock first?"

I didn't actually consider his question before I nodded and pushed myself out of the water. It was cold—*really* freaking cold—but the thought was forced to the back of my mind when Liam didn't hesitate to drag my briefs down and grip my cock.

He directed it toward his mouth and looked down at my erection like he'd never seen anything more delicious. Lapping at the precum beading at my crown, he moaned and slid his mouth around me.

"Oh, fuck," I cried, gripping the sides of the hot tub to keep myself from falling backward. His mouth was unrelenting and perfectly warm as he pushed me deep and nudged the back of his throat until he gagged. He didn't let up, though. He held my cock deep and pushed deeper and deeper until I could feel the beginning of my orgasm drawing up my balls.

"Stop, stop, stop," I muttered. I speared my hand into the back of his hair and yanked hard. He popped off, spit collecting around his dark blond stubble, and a tired smile lifted his lips. "Are you trying to make me come before we get to the really good stuff?"

His mouth tilted higher. "You're saying this isn't the really good stuff?"

"You know what I mean," I groaned as he twisted his hand up and down my soaking shaft.

"Oh, shit." I swung my head to the left and in the direction of the voice. Palmer was standing in the faint light streaming outside from our room. She was barefoot, her robe wrapped tightly around her, and she tossed the rest of her french fry into her mouth. "I didn't mean to interrupt."

"You could never interrupt, Sparky," Liam murmured before I shoved his mouth back over me while I smiled at my wife, whose eyes went wide with arousal. I fucked up into Liam's waiting, eager mouth as my eyes bounced between the man in front of me and the woman watching us both.

"You two are so hot," she muttered, taking a step closer as the wind whipped around us. She tightened her robe around her and folded her arms to keep it closed. "And I want to keep watching, but it's fucking freezing."

I let Liam's hair go, and he pulled off, wiping his spit on the back of his hand.

"Let's go." I grabbed his hand and tugged us out of the pool, reaching for his towel and tossing it back at him. He caught it with a chuckle, and we both stripped off our wet clothes before we stepped inside. Palmer ran to the bathroom, probably to grab another towel, but we'd warm up eventually. I didn't want to wait another second.

"I love the foreplay," I said as Liam pumped my cock and kissed down the side of my neck. "But I need you inside me now."

"Lube?" he asked, and I nodded, pointing to the bedside table. We both looked in that direction, and he kissed me once more before he instructed, "Sit down on the edge of the bed."

I did exactly as he asked, dropping down onto the bed as Palmer strode back into the room. Her eyes bounced from me to Liam, then back to me. She tossed the towel on the bed and met Liam in front of me as he flipped the lube bottle open.

She pressed her hands to his chest and tilted her head back to look up at him. His eyes were soft as he stared down at her, and his cock kicked when her fingers brushed slightly lower, and she took another step closer.

"Are you going to fuck your boyfriend?" she asked.

He hummed and leaned down to press his lips to hers. "I am. What do you think about that, Sparky?"

Palmer smiled and pressed up onto her toes. She steadied her hands on his pecs and positioned her mouth next to his ear. I couldn't hear what she said or read her lips, but I saw Liam's small smile. Then he scooped her up and whispered something back to her. She giggled, a beautiful, sweet sound, and he set her back down on her feet.

He kissed her soundly, and she melted into him in front of my eyes.

She crossed to me and kissed me too. Then she crawled onto the bed and settled on her knees behind me, wrapping her arms around my neck as Liam stepped in front of me.

"You're going to take his cock so well," she murmured into my ear.

"Yes, he is," Liam agreed. "Now, lean back. Lay in her lap while I get you ready for me." Palmer urged me back and positioned my head in her lap. She combed her fingers through my hair, and she smiled down at me.

"Feet on the bed, baby. Open your legs for me," Liam instructed, and apparently, I liked being bossed around a little bit because the command in his voice made me want to do whatever he said.

So I did. I planted my feet on the edge of the mattress and spread my legs.

Liam reached down and grasped my hips, tugging me closer to the edge, and Palmer followed us, keeping my head in her lap. Her legs were the perfect pillow, and her soothing touch through my hair was centering.

Liam dropped the lube bottle on the bed next to me and reached down between my legs. He pushed my cheeks apart and stared at the place he was about to fuck. He gazed down at me as he tied half of his blond hair back in a short bun.

"Such a good little hole," he muttered, then dropped to his knees, which was such a shame because I couldn't watch him stare down at me like I was everything he'd wanted, but it was also amazing when I felt his tongue against my "good little hole," as he called it.

I cursed under my breath, and my back arched. He traced the rim of my ass with his tongue and licked up until he sucked one of my balls. Pleasure speared through me as I felt his tongue against my sack.

Dropping back down, he pushed his tongue into my ass and ate me like he'd never tasted anything better, just like how he'd eaten Palmer that morning.

It had been a long time since I'd felt pleasure so acute in that area, but Liam was doing the perfect job of reminding me why I loved it so much.

"Liam," I groaned, and he stood up with a smile on his face.

"I know, baby. No more foreplay. I'll get my cock in you soon enough. Now, spread your legs wider."

He grabbed the lube bottle and flipped the lid, while I gripped behind my thighs, right at the curve of my knee, and pulled them back.

"Good job," he murmured and took a step forward. Palmer ran one hand through my hair while the other massaged down my arm and over my chest. Then Liam tapped a lubed finger against my hole, and with the two of them touching me at the same time, I couldn't imagine anything better.

"Relax for me, baby," Liam muttered, and I did my best. I let out a deep breath, and Palmer leaned forward, kissing me softly as Liam pushed one strong finger inside me.

It didn't hurt, but it was slightly uncomfortable for a few minutes. That was until my body acclimated to the new sensation, and the discomfort morphed into pleasure.

"More," I begged, and Liam didn't say anything. He just dripped more lube on his hand and added another finger. Sliding the second thick digit in slowly, Liam's jaw went slack, and I gasped.

Palmer continued her gentle, soothing ministrations through my hair and down my chest, but with the second finger, she began whispering encouragement.

"You're doing such a good job."

"You can take more."

"Bear down on his fingers. Doesn't it feel so good?"

And I did exactly as she instructed. I squeezed around Liam's fingers, and I appreciated his hearty groan. I made the mistake of laughing, though, because a second later, he hooked his fingers forward and grazed my prostate. Stars erupted behind my eyes, and I let go of my legs, pressing my feet on the bed and trying to thrust his fingers deeper inside me.

"This is taking too long," I growled. "Just get inside me." Arousal was pounding through me, swimming through my bloodstream like it was the only sustenance I needed to keep me alive.

Liam slammed a strong palm down on the inside of one of my thighs and shook his head.

"I don't want to hurt you—"

"I don't care," I threw back at him. "I can handle a little bit of pain, but I need you."

His eyes shot to mine, and I tried to plead with him. Strength and dominance rolled off him in waves, and I wanted to feel every part of that. Just as I opened my mouth to start begging, he moved.

He withdrew his fingers and reached for the bottle again. Leaning forward, I couldn't miss seeing him dribble the liquid on his thick, erect cock. He smeared it up and down his shaft, the sound so fucking obscene, and the sight even better.

He stalked toward me, clean hand pushing my thigh back, still stroking his cock. "What do you think, Sparky? Do you want to suck his cock while I push into his ass?"

My eyes shuttered closed with the mental image, but I felt Palmer's enthusiastic nod before she slipped out from behind me. My head hit the bed beneath me, and I cracked my eyes open when I felt the bed dip beside me. She tossed her robe aside, left in her cute, cotton gray matching bra and panty set.

She gave me a lustful look tinged with wicked intent, then leaned forward and licked up the underside of my hard length. That was the moment Liam pressed his thick head against my ass, and I gasped at the overwhelming sensations.

twenty

. . .

Palmer

I SPIT on Easton's cock and pumped hard with my hand as I watched Liam slowly push into his ass.

"Relax, baby," Liam murmured, and I looked at my husband. His eyes were scrunched close, and I knew how he felt. I had experienced the same pleasure and pain tumbling through him many times before.

It felt like an immense amount of pressure, and it wasn't the most comfortable sensation. But I knew the pleasure that would follow, especially since it was Liam who was fucking him.

His eyes still closed, I kissed Easton, then I dragged my tongue across his lips. He parted for me and groaned into my mouth. My hand pumped in easy, rhythmic strokes down his cock, and slowly the tension dissolved. His lips effortlessly slipped against mine, and he began to jerk up into my waiting hand.

I kissed East one last time and straightened, immediately looking down at where Liam disappeared inside him. More than half his cock was poised inside East, and I stretched for Liam.

He captured me with an unforgiving grip in my hair and

kissed me long and hard. Such a carnal kiss compared to Easton's, and I loved them both equally. The hard and soft of it, the contradiction was breathtaking.

Easton moaned, and I broke off the kiss, dropping my mouth on his throbbing cock. I sucked in long, hard pulls, just the way I knew Easton liked it. But the whole time, I kept a watchful eye on Liam, pushing inside him.

I could feel the tension and desire climbing with every subsequent inch, and finally, when Liam's hips pressed against Easton's ass, and there wasn't a breath left between them, it snapped.

"Fuck me," Easton barked. Sweat beaded on his forehead, and every muscle in his stomach and arms flexed.

Liam didn't wait. He pulled out and shoved back in. *Hard.* Easton slid up the bed with the force, but Liam gripped his hips and tugged him back down. His strokes were long and hard, and I dropped my mouth back down on Easton's dick. The impressive amount of precum collecting at his tip was salty, and I pushed him to the back of my throat.

Liam's brutal thrusts pushed Easton's cock deeper into my mouth, and all I had to do was sit there and take it. I gagged, spit dripping down the side of him.

Closing my eyes, I listened to the erotic sounds we made together, the arousing symphony of writhing, passionate bodies. Fingers twisted in the back of my hair, and without opening my eyes, I knew it was Easton. He held my head in place, with only enough pressure that I knew he wanted me to stay exactly where I was.

"Yes, you feel so good," Liam groaned, and I dropped my hand between my body and the bed, pushing my panties to the side and rubbing my swollen clit.

I moaned around Easton's dick, and he bucked harder into my mouth with the vibration from the sound. Another hand—Liam's—smoothed down my back, and I opened my eyes, popping off Easton to look up at him. The lust made his eyes dark, and I wanted to be swallowed whole by it.

He watched me as his hand continued lower and slipped against my drenched pussy. He pushed one finger inside, and my moan was guttural and pure. He fucked me with that finger in time with his thrusts in and out of East. And god, it felt so good, I started to fuck back onto him. One finger turned to two, and I struggled to keep my eyes open.

I didn't want to miss a moment of the action in front of me. Liam's brow was furrowed, and a sheen of sweat coated his broad chest. My eyes dipped lower to that defined V created by his lower ab muscles that pointed directly to one of my favorite appendages ever.

Every muscle was working overtime as he fucked my husband, and Easton was struggling to keep his legs open. His strong, muscular thighs tensed as he panted, and he took everything Liam gave him. Watching the ecstasy cross his perfect features, I wanted more.

Pressing up onto my knees, Liam's fingers slipped free as I tugged my bra off over my head and slipped my panties down my legs. With both of their eyes on me, I considered my next move and contemplated the best way to make it happen. I shivered under their attention and the raw, naked desire burning in their eyes.

"What—" Easton asked as Liam's movements slowed. I swung my leg over Easton's hips, facing Liam. The position was a little awkward at first, but I scooted my hips forward and planted one hand behind me and next to Easton's stomach.

I glanced over my shoulder at Easton, and my long hair brushed lightly against his chest. "I'm going to ride your cock while our boyfriend fucks you. Is that okay with you?"

"God, yes," he groaned, reaching forward and wrapping his big hands around the smallest part of my waist. "I need you so bad." And it wasn't usual to hear Easton beg, but I loved how it sounded. I loved the rough, pleading quality of his voice and how he'd willingly given himself to the endless amounts of pleasure Liam and I together could create.

Smiling at my husband, I turned back around. My pussy grazed the tip of Easton's pulsing cock, and I wanted nothing more than to sink directly down on it.

"That okay with you, Liam?"

"More than okay, sweet girl. Let me help you."

In the position I was in, it would have been a challenge, yet manageable, to position Easton's cock so I could slip down on it. But Liam slipped in and out of Easton in easy, leisurely rolls and was able to guide Easton's cock to my pussy.

I felt him notch at my opening, and he instructed me to, "Sink down. Take him all."

Easton groaned heartily behind me as I did what he said. I reveled in the stretch of Easton's thick shaft. No matter how many times we had sex, it always took a second for me to get used to it. It always felt a little too much for a moment, but I loved the stretch.

"It's so pretty, how well you take him," Liam muttered. His eyes were locked on where Easton's fat cock stretched my pussy. "Such a good fucking girl for us. So perfect."

Easton's hands slid down my hips and squeezed hard. I planted my other hand behind me and ground down onto Easton. I couldn't move much, but I quickly realized that didn't matter. With me impaled on Easton's cock, Liam's easy, measured thrusts grew harder, and each time he pushed in, it shoved Easton deeper inside me.

Liam fucking Easton essentially made it possible for Easton to fuck me.

His thick length shunted in and out of me, and I could feel his deep groans of pleasure against my back. With every thrust, Easton's hands tightened around my hips, and I hoped his hold would leave behind marks that would last awhile.

My mouth dropped open in ecstasy as he hit the perfect spot that made pleasure shoot through me. My eyes locked with Liam's tumultuous hazel ones.

One of his hands wrapped around Easton's thigh, his other

massaged my breast, twisting my nipple in his calloused grip before running his thumb over the sensitive peak.

With desire slipping through every inch of my body, I lifted my left hand and offered my fingers to Liam. He knew what I wanted and sucked my first three fingers into his mouth. Liam's eyes shuttered closed for a moment as his tongue lapped around each digit, teasing me like he did Easton's cock, and I clenched around my husband.

"Fuck," Easton groaned. "You two are going to make me come. It feels too good. Oh, fuck, *harder*."

Liam let my fingers go with a smile and fixed his hand around my throat as I rubbed my clit. My body was greedy for the orgasm, and it was just right there. With the extra stimulation and two men on either side of me, I knew it wouldn't be long until I shattered.

"We should let our girl come first," Liam growled. He tightened his hold on my throat, and I leaned in the best I could. I couldn't find the words, but I tried to communicate with my eyes how I wanted more pressure. I wanted his fingers to nearly cut off my airway.

My message received, he clamped his hand down harder, and a smile slipped over my lips. With the lack of oxygen, my mind fixed on only the purposeful and deep desire.

My fingers never stopped moving over my clit, and Easton's hold on me guided me up and down his ever-thickening cock. The tension was electric, and I could feel his orgasm cresting just as mine was.

We were all panting breaths and grappling hands. We were slaves to the pleasure and could do nothing but surrender.

"Come on, sweet girl," Liam grunted through clenched teeth. Some of the blond hair had fallen from his hair tie, and I knew he was just barely able to hold off his own orgasm. "Let me watch you come. I want to see you come."

"Show Liam how pretty you are when you shatter," Easton

murmured behind me. "Give in, baby. Show him how you come. Give in."

"Don't stop," was the one broken plea I managed.

"We won't stop," they both said.

"We're never going to stop," Easton growled.

"I'm watching, sweet girl. I'm watching, and we're never going to stop."

My vision began to darken at the edges, and my breath caught in my throat. Then deep-seated, all-consuming pleasure wracked my body in never-ending waves. I was clenching and writhing, trying to keep myself sitting up.

"There she is," I heard Liam murmur somewhere that sounded distant. "So fucking beautiful."

Liam's hand disappeared, and I opened my eyes long enough to watch his head fall back. A few more strong, unforgiving thrusts, and Liam shouted his release, pumping into Easton, who had finally given in himself. I felt his orgasm hot and deep, and I slipped down even farther over him.

It was several seconds—maybe a minute or two, I don't know, I lost count—until I could think straight again.

"Lay back, baby," Easton muttered and tugged me backward. Slowly, I lowered myself back on top of him and kicked my legs out so I wasn't twisted up like a damn pretzel. He willingly accepted my weight, and I rested my head on his chest.

Easton looked past me to Liam and motioned him to lean down. "Come here, but don't pull out," Easton requested.

Liam ran a hand over his face, shining with sweat, and pushed his hair back. He leaned forward and squeezed me between their two large, hard bodies. Easton clasped a hand around the back of Liam's neck and guided him into a languid sort of kiss. The one of two lovers finally at peace with their feelings. Their tongues caressed each other's, and I watched in excited fascination.

They both turned to me. Liam kissed me first, then guided

my face to Easton's. I adjusted to my left so we had a better angle and kissed Easton.

My heart lightened when Liam's lips joined ours, and we were consumed by a three-way kiss. Tongues and teeth and lips—it was perfect.

After a few minutes, my neck ached, and I dropped back down onto Easton's chest. We were all smiling, fully satisfied and happy.

"My curiosity is going to kill me," Easton said. His left hand dragged up and down my side while his other still held the back of Liam's neck. "What did you whisper to him earlier?"

I giggled, and Liam's smile widened before he dropped his face into the crook of my neck.

"I told him that I couldn't wait to watch him fuck you. That I couldn't wait to see the two men I love together."

It would have been so much harder not to tell Liam that I was in love with him. I'd spent years holding those feelings close to my chest. I didn't want to keep them a secret for a second longer.

"And I told her that I, of course, love her too." We smiled through another deep kiss and looked back at Easton.

I could count on one hand the number of times I'd seen my husband cry—the day he proposed, the day we got married, and when we watched *Marley & Me* for the first time. And I could add this exact moment to the short list.

His eyes welled with tears as he glanced between us.

"East, I—" Liam started, but Easton shook his head and cupped his cheek.

"I love you both so fucking much. So much it doesn't feel real," Easton explained, and I nuzzled into his neck, kissing his warm skin. "I've never felt so…complete."

"I know what you mean, but it is real," Liam explained. "And it's just so fucking perfect."

epilogue

. . .

Liam

Six months later

I SLIPPED my key into the lock and pushed our front door open. After a long day, I felt the stress drain from me as it always did when I came home to them.

We'd gotten back from our life-changing vacation, and I knew they were right—I couldn't go back to living separate lives. I wanted to be with them as much as I could. I'd moved in when my lease ended a month later, but we all wanted a fresh start for the three of us—a new place to start our new relationship.

So we bought a new house not far away, one that we all picked out together that would be our forever home.

Walking through the entryway and boxes still lining the walls, I smiled at the sight before me. Easton was standing at the stove, stirring something that was destined to taste amazing, while Palmer was perched on the large island in the middle of the kitchen.

The light from the setting sun shone through the windows at the back of the house, and the puppy we'd adopted, Peanut Butter, or Butter for short, bounded through the grass I definitely needed to mow that weekend.

"Thank God you're finally home," Palmer exclaimed, spinning to look at me. "We can't decide on what movie to watch tonight. East wants to watch this new rom-com, and I'm more in the mood for horror."

Shaking my head, I dropped my bag by the barstool and rounded the island. Palmer opened her arms, silently requesting a hug, but I shook my head.

"I'm sweaty and disgusting. I seriously need a shower."

She tilted her head and narrowed her eyes, tucking a piece of her long brown hair behind her ear. "I don't give a shit," she argued. "Are you really going to deny me?"

I chuckled and closed the short distance between us. I stepped between her legs and tugged her quickly to the edge. She wrapped her arms around my neck, and I snaked mine around her back.

"God, you do stink," Easton quipped from behind me, but still placed a kiss on the other side of my neck and ran a hand down my spine. I could hear the laughter in his voice.

"Sorry, we can't all work in an air-conditioned office all day," I joked back, and he slapped my ass for good measure.

"I kind of like the way you smell after a hard day at work," Palmer said. She slipped her fingers through my hair and tugged lightly. I pulled back, and she kissed me. More stress and anxiety slipped away with the easy brush of her lips and Easton's presence at my back.

"I thought we had family dinner tonight?" I asked, but Palmer shook her head.

"No, we're having dinner with them tomorrow night."

We were having Palmer and Easton's families over for dinner, as well as a few of our friends. We liked to get everyone together as often as possible. And we were lucky—everyone had accepted us with open arms. We also had a lot to celebrate.

We bought a new house, and Evin, Palmer's sister, had hit a career milestone she'd been working toward. They also wanted us to meet Evin's best friend, Aiden's, new boyfriend.

Evin was oddly very excited about the pairing.

"If that's the case, maybe we do the horror movie, *then* the rom-com, so we can all actually sleep tonight."

Palmer smiled and kissed me once more. "And that's why we needed you here to make a decision."

I spun around and was immediately greeted by Easton's lop-sided grin. He gripped my hips and pulled me forward, pressing our bodies together and placing a searing kiss on my lips.

"I missed you today," he muttered, drawing back to look at me.

"I miss you every day," I admitted. "Both of you." I threw a smile over my shoulder that Palmer easily returned. Fuck, they were all I ever needed. The three of us together were…just perfect.

"Okay, so two movies," Palmer announced. "When will dinner be ready, East?"

Easton spun around and eyed the sauce on the stove. "Probably thirty minutes."

"Perfect. Just enough time for a quick shower," she said, jumping off the counter and lacing her fingers through mine. "And for a quickie too."

I laughed and caught Easton shaking his head out of the corner of my eye. She dragged me toward the stairs, but East grabbed my other hand and kissed me again, a kiss that I felt everywhere and made my cock stir behind my jeans.

"Fine, but don't wear him out too much. I have big plans for us tonight."

Palmer and I looked at each other excitedly, and she promised we would still have enough energy for anything he had planned. Because Easton's plans were always worth it, and the three of us together were unbelievable.

I loved them so much. They were my home. Always had been, and now, always would be.

THE END

acknowledgments

This book was so fun, and honestly, one of the easiest to write. Most books aren't simple, but this story unfolded so easily. Honestly, I think it took me less than two weeks to write. For me, that's insane!

I knew I wanted to write another throuple, and Easton, Liam, and Palmer were exactly everything I'd hoped and more.

The point of this series is to celebrate love in all its forms. And I think their dynamic is so special and pure. It was the culmination of years of secret feelings and longing.

Friends-to-lovers might be one of my favorite tropes to write; however, there was also something so fun about exploring the dynamic of a happily married couple. Easton and Palmer were *SO* happy together, but without Liam, they knew something, or better yet someone, was missing.

As always, thank you so much to my amazing alpha and beta readers. And to My Brother's Editor for making my words sparkle.

Mayhem Cover Creations never delivers a cover that is anything less than perfect 😉 See what I did there!

And thank you to my incredible readers! There's so much more to come!

also by grace turner

If you love this book, check out Grace Turner's other books. All available on Amazon and with Kindle Unlimited: https://amazon.com/author/graceturner

And to stay up to date on everything else Grace has to come, sign up for her newsletter at graceturnerauthor.com and make sure to check out:

instagram.com/graceturnerauthor
facebook.com/graceturnerauthor
tiktok.com/@graceturnerauthor
goodreads.com/graceturner

about the author

Grace Turner lives in Houston, Texas with her husband and two rambunctious pups and has a revolving door full of friends and family always visiting. By day, she works as a paralegal, and by night she reads, writes, and breathes contemporary romance

www.ingramcontent.com/pod-product-compliance
Lightning Source LLC
LaVergne TN
LVHW010623100826
845148LV00014B/3086

* 9 7 9 8 9 8 7 6 2 2 5 7 5 *